RIBBON
the Border Collie
From Herder to Healer

By Lyn Bezek

Illustrations
by Su Hand

WESTERN REFLECTIONS
PUBLISHING COMPANY®
Lake City, Colorado

ISBN 978-1-932738-51-3
Library of Congress Control Number: 2008924525

First Edition
Printed in the United States of America

Illustrations © 2008 by Su Hand
Cover and text design by Laurie Goralka Design

Western Reflections Publishing Company®
P.O. Box 1149
Lake City, CO 81235
www.westernreflectionspub.com

For my niece and nephew,
*the **real** Allison and James.*
May they use every single bit of the talent
God gave them.

 Allison could already tell Ribbon had the makings of a champion. The six-month-old Border Collie pup, ears standing at attention and muscles tensed, strained against Allison's arms as they sat in the grandstands watching the Meeker Classic Sheepdog Championship Trials.

Ever since Allison had looked into the intelligent, chocolate brown eyes of the little puppy for the very first time, she had felt an uncanny connection, almost as if Ribbon could read her mind. And she was absolutely sure the dog could understand things about this world she as a human could never know.

She had named the dog Ribbon because of the alternating ribbons of black and white fur that started at the black tip of each ear and ended with a white stripe at the very tip of her feathery tail.

Allison's mother, Gwen, gave that tail an affectionate pull as she slid in to sit beside Allison and Ribbon on the bleachers. "Your brother and Spirit are up next, Allison." Pride and excitement showed in her voice. "I sure hope they get some cooperative sheep."

Just then, Allison saw her older brother, James, take his place in the field straight ahead of them. At his side was Ribbon's father, Spirit, a lean and beautiful Border Collie whose shiny black coat glistened in the afternoon sunlight. Unlike Ribbon, the only white fur on Spirit was a large heart-shaped tuft on his upper chest.

Allison smiled to herself as she watched her brother and his dog get ready to go through their paces. From the day four years ago when James had brought Spirit home from the Belcher ranch next to theirs, the boy and dog had been inseparable. They had played together, slept together, and trained hard together. Spirit always seemed to anticipate James' every wish—a skill that should stand him in good stead for today's herding competition.

On cue, James gave a shrill whistle that sent Spirit racing uphill through rugged ravines and around clumps of sagebrush until he circled expertly behind the group of frisky sheep that had been released at the far top of the field. The crowd of onlookers broke out in applause as Spirit quietly and confidently herded the sheep in an almost perfect straight line toward James and then steadily guided them behind him toward the first of three sets of gates. "Look, Ribbon! Your dad is doing great so far." Allison bent her face to snuggle Ribbon's soft ear. The puppy kept watching the proceedings intently, her small body leaning forward in Allison's lap.

"Maybe you and Ribbon will be out there competing someday." Gwen smiled in her daughter's direction.

"No maybes about it," Allison said firmly, turning toward Gwen to emphasize her point. "I already know in my heart that Ribbon is destined to be a herding champion one day."

A loud groan that rose up suddenly from the crowd refocused Allison's and her mother's attention on Spirit. One especially stubborn sheep had bolted in the opposite direction from the rest of the pack, and Spirit was doing his level best to bring it back to the fold. He accomplished the task in just a few minutes, but Allison knew the judges would subtract points from Spirit's overall score for this little detour. She watched to see if this would cause James or his dog to lose their concentration, but both appeared to continue on undaunted, with Spirit flawlessly following his master's whistled commands. As the dog guided all the sheep into a rectangular pen and James quickly swung the gate closed, appreciative applause echoed off the surrounding hills.

Allison and Ribbon hurried to meet James and Spirit as they came off the course. "Good boy, Spirit! Good job!" Allison cooed as she and Ribbon flopped down beside the panting dog on a wide patch of grass. James, looking dejected, joined them, stretching his long legs out in front of him on the ground. Their score hadn't been posted yet, but he already knew that he and Spirit would not make the cut for the semi-finals tomorrow.

"You two looked great out there," Allison said, but James shook his head.

"We were on a roll until that one wayward sheep decided to make a U turn," he said. "Things can change in an instant, that's for sure."

Gwen came up behind James and gave him a warm hug, then placed a big metal bowl of water in front of Spirit, who gulped it down in a few seconds, leaving only a few drops in the bottom for Ribbon to lap up. Allison refilled the bowl from her canteen.

Gwen settled herself cross-legged on the ground next to James. "Your dad says the sheep in Meeker are the feistiest of any herding competition anywhere, so don't be too hard on yourself. You and Spirit should be very proud of what you were able to do out there."

"Why are the Meeker sheep so tough, Mom?" asked Allison, stroking the white tuft on Spirit's chest. Ribbon nipped at Spirit's outstretched front paw, trying to get him to play, but Spirit only opened one eye then closed it again.

"These sheep have just spent all summer up in high mountain pastures where nobody—human or dog—has bothered them, so they're not in any mood to be herded. That makes them particularly challenging." Gwen paused to brush a bothersome fly away from her face before continuing. "Plus, as you kids already know, this competition draws the top 120 dogs and handlers in North America, which makes competing here even more of a challenge. James, you and Spirit really held your own out there today. You're both winners in my book."

"I guess you're right, Mom." James signaled for Spirit to come to him. The dog immediately stood up, stretched, then walked over and gave James a lick on the cheek. "Even though we didn't make it to the top twenty, we gave it our all, didn't we, boy?"

Ribbon chose that moment to leap on Spirit's back, and the two dogs went tumbling down the hill.

"Is anybody else hungry?" asked Allison.

"Yes," Gwen answered, standing up and brushing off her jeans. "Let's go get something to eat at one of the food booths, then pack up the truck. We have a long drive ahead of us."

"I'll race you to the hot dog stand!" Allison challenged her brother.

Suddenly more hungry than tired, James jumped up and took off like he was shot out of a cannon, with his sister in hot pursuit. Gwen and the two startled dogs were left to bring up the rear.

On the long drive home, Allison laid on her back next to the side window in the pickup's camper so she could watch the brilliant blanket of stars gradually spread overhead in the clear Colorado sky as darkness settled over the landscape. Spirit stretched out his tired body next to James, but Ribbon, wide awake after a short nap, sat on Allison's belly and stared out at the stars too.

Allison reached up and took Ribbon's furry face in her hands. "You know, girl, if we train really, really hard, I feel it in my bones that you could be Top Dog in all of North America someday. There's no reason we shouldn't shoot for the stars!"

Ribbon let out a high-pitched bark, then drew up the corners of her mouth in what looked for all the world like a Border Collie smile.

 For the next two years, Allison and Ribbon, with the willing help of James and Spirit, spent every possible moment after school and on weekends turning Ribbon into an expert herding dog. Ribbon was an eager and enthusiastic student and, true to her Border Collie work ethic, would herd the ranch's cattle, sheep, and goats until she dropped, if Allison had let her.

"Border Collies were bred to work," James had stressed to his sister when Ribbon was still a puppy. "They love nothing better than to herd—it's in their blood—but it's up to you as her trainer and protector to make sure she doesn't overdo it and ruin her health."

Tears had welled up in Allison's big green eyes at the thought of any harm coming to her precious, precocious puppy. "Oh, James!" she had exclaimed. "I will never work Ribbon too hard. I want her to be a champion, yes; but she's also my best friend. I'll always love and care for her with every ounce of my being!"

James, who had been Allison's protector since the day she was born, had smiled down at his sister. Despite the six years between their ages, they had always been very close. "I know that, Sis. I just want you to know about the true nature of this breed of dog. Border Collies are smart and energetic and they definitely need to have a purpose in life. But they can easily become workaholics, and that's never a good thing—for man or beast."

As Ribbon's training progressed, Allison took James' advice to heart and made sure Ribbon got plenty of doggy downtime each day. That meant games of catch with a much-gnawed Frisbee, multiple belly rubs, and long, luxurious snoozes draped over Allison's legs while she did her homework on the sofa. But the best time of all came at night—after all the chores of the day were done—when girl and dog would sit side by side on the back steps and watch the moon come up over the tops of the mountains that rimmed the ranch to the south.

One winter night, the shimmering stars looked so bright and close that Allison felt she could scoop a big handful of them from the sky and sprinkle them on Ribbon's bedtime biscuit and in her own mug of hot chocolate. "Wouldn't it be awesome if we could actually eat stars so we could always shine?" she murmured.

Allison caught a glimpse of her dog out of the corner of her eye and started to laugh. Ribbon was looking directly at her, the corners of her mouth turned up in her famous smile. "I guess you don't need to eat any stars, you silly dog. You shine already, don't you?" Ribbon let out a sharp little yip and nodded her head up and down. "You are my star!" Allison happily hugged the dog with all her might. "You are definitely my star!"

Chapter 3

On the last day of the school year, Allison's father and mother scheduled a family meeting for after dinner. Gwen poured four tall glasses of her special iced raspberry tea and set the pitcher on the kitchen table as soon as she heard Allison and James noisily coming through the back door after finishing their evening chores.

After a few minutes, their dad, Tim, came in from the barn, taking off his mud-caked cowboy boots before sitting down in his stockinged feet. "I have a proposition for you two kids for this summer," he began, looking across the table at his children to make sure he had their undivided attention. "It would pay well, plus give Ribbon some good herding experience before the Meeker Sheepdog Trials in September." Spirit and Ribbon trotted into the room and settled in under the table as Tim continued. "I got a call from Rick Moser over in Frisco yesterday, and he asked if our goats were available through the summer to eat the noxious weeds that are crowding out the normal vegetation all over Summit County. I told him I'd have to check with you two before I promised anything. You and the dogs would have to camp out right next to the goats and move the herd from place to place every couple of days."

"That sounds great, but who would help with all the chores around here if Allison and I are gone all the time?" asked James, running his hands through the thatch of dark hair that always hung defiantly over his forehead.

Tim took a sip of his tea. "The Belchers have an extra hired hand they have no work for at the moment. He has offered to come over here if we need him."

"Plus, I'm going to be working less shifts at the hospital this summer so I can pick up some of the slack," Gwen interjected. "And I'd plan to bring you some home-cooked meals from time to time so you two wouldn't get tired of your own camp cooking."

"Just like Meals on Wheels!" exclaimed Allison, who often helped her mother deliver hot meals from the school cafeteria to homebound senior citizens on the weekend.

"That's right, but you two wouldn't be homebound, just goatbound," Gwen laughed.

"So what do you think, you two?" Tim asked, looking first at James then Allison. "It will be a lot of work, and it will tie you down for the whole summer. That's the down side. But it pays extremely well, and Spirit and Ribbon—not to mention the goats—would have the time of their lives. That's the up side."

Joy bubbled up inside Allison. This was a dream come true. She couldn't think of a more wonderful way to spend the coming summer—hanging out with her big brother, sleeping under the stars, and getting uninterrupted training time with her dog.

Allison looked at James. James looked at Allison. Both broke into big grins. Suddenly, two furry heads appeared above the checkered tablecloth. Spirit gave a short, happy howl. Ribbon simply smiled.

"Well," chuckled Tim. "I'll take that as a yes all around."

The next few days were a frenzy of activity for everyone at the Colby ranch. Tim changed the oil in the old but sturdy pickup truck, then took it to his trusted mechanic Jed in Silverthorne for a tuneup and overall checkup. Gwen did major grocery shopping for camping staples and snacks, then spent one entire day in the kitchen whipping up pots of stews and soups, baking dozens of chewy oatmeal raisin cookies, and concocting her own recipe for healthy doggy granola. James packed up the tent, the camp stove, bedrolls, extra blankets, clothes for all kinds of weather, and his favorite battered guitar. Then he did a quick exam of each goat in their herd to make sure all were healthy and up to the challenge ahead. Allison packed her things in a giant duffel bag—jeans, tee shirts, sweatshirts, and a heavy jacket plus a few mystery novels and her trusty camera that went everywhere with her. Then she packed the dogs' things in a bright red daypack—two Frisbees, leashes, brushes, water and food bowls, and lots of chew toys.

Finally everything was packed and ready to go.

Monday dawned cool and clear, a typical early June morning in the Rocky Mountains. Tim and James, along with the two dogs, eager and excited at the prospect of going for a ride, expertly herded the nervous goats into the back of the trailer. James had just securely slammed the tailgate shut when Gwen and Allison came down the back porch steps carrying a large cooler between them. Tim pushed up the truck seat and easily hoisted the cooler behind it, next to two giant bags of dogfood.

"Well, looks like none of you will be starving any time soon!" Tim remarked, giving Allison a boost up into the truck. Ribbon and Spirit quickly jumped in and settled themselves on the seat beside her, then looked around impatiently as if to say, "Let's get this show on the road."

After hugs were given all around, James, a cowboy hat pulled down over his unruly hair, climbed in behind the steering wheel and started the engine. "Okay, everyone, fasten your seatbelts. Let the adventure begin."

"We'll come see you soon!" Gwen shouted after them as the truck and trailer rattled away down the lane. She turned toward her husband, a worried look on her face. "You don't think the kids are too young to take on a job like this, do you?"

Tim put his arm around her waist as they walked toward the house. "I have a lot of faith in those two kids—and those two dogs. They'll be just fine," he assured her, opening the screen door for her. "Now I hope you saved at least a couple of those oatmeal raisin cookies for me."

Chapter 4

As they drove past postcard-pretty ranchland toward the town of Silverthorne, Allison asked James if they could take the long way around Lake Dillon and stop at her favorite place in Summit County—a popular overlook called Sapphire Point. James argued that it would take too much gas and time, but Allison begged and begged.

The truth was Sapphire Point was James' favorite spot too. A short hike down a dirt path led to a clearing rimmed by immense boulders. From there you could look down on the placid blue waters of Lake Dillon, which stretched from the community of Frisco at one end to the resort town of Dillon on the other end. "Breathtaking" was the only word that adequately described the view. Sometimes, when James was depressed or confused or just had a problem he had to think through, he would come to Sapphire Point and silently soak in its serenity and beauty. It always made him feel better.

So, after they drove through Silverthorne, instead of turning on Dillon Dam Road, James kept the truck pointing uphill. That's when Allison realized she had won the battle. Within a few minutes they had turned on to Swan Mountain Road and reached the Sapphire Point parking lot. Allison grabbed her camera from her duffel bag and jumped out of the truck, the two dogs following joyously at her heels. "We'll meet you down there," she called over her shoulder to her brother, who was checking the tailgate on the trailer to make sure the goats stayed put.

"Oh, look at that view!" Allison cried. Ribbon and Spirit obliged by scampering up on the largest boulder and craning their furry necks at the scene below them. Allison snapped a photo of them from behind, making a mental note to consider that shot—if it turned out as cute as she thought it would—for a future Christmas card.

"Hey, Sis," James said, coming up behind her. "We need to put these mutts on leashes since this is a public area." He handed Allison Ribbon's pink leash then hooked a blue leash to Spirit's collar.

Just then, a tiny striped creature ran in front of them and disappeared over the top of a stone wall. Both dogs whined softly and stared in that direction.

"Calm down, you guys," James clucked at them, as he and Allison walked over and sat down on the wall, keeping the two excited dogs close by their sides. Peering over the rocks that tumbled down the mountainside beyond the wall, they could see at least a dozen busy chipmunks scurrying in and out of the crevices between the rocks.

"I bet our intrepid Border Collies would like to herd those little rodents," laughed James, pulling a bag of sunflower seeds from his jeans pocket and showering a handful down over the hungry chipmunks. The seeds were consumed in an instant.

Allison patted the dogs' heads, as both of them, bodies tensed, watched the scene below with intense interest. "If you two dogs lost your footing on those rocks, you'd both end up in Lake Dillon," she said. "And it's a long way down." Suddenly suspicious, she looked over at her brother. "Hey, how come you happened to bring these sunflower seeds along for the chipmunks if you were so dead set against stopping at Sapphire Point?" she asked, digging into his bag and scattering more seeds down over the rocks. "You intended to come here all along, didn't you?"

"Well, little sister, I guess I just like to hear you beg." A satisfied grin crept over James' face.

"Creep!" she replied, hitting him playfully on the shoulder.

For the next few minutes brother and sister were quiet, content to gaze at the incredibly beautiful vista before them. The two dogs never took their eyes off the chipmunks.

"Someday I'm going to get married at this very spot," Allison said dreamily.

"I doubt that!"

James' comment snapped Allison out of her reverie. "Oh, and why do you doubt that?" she demanded. "Lots of people have their weddings here."

"Because first there has to be a groom, and I don't see you finding one of those very easily," he teased.

"Why, you utter creep!" Allison lunged at James, knocking him off balance as her hands tightened around his neck. "Take that back, you moron!" she shouted as the two of them wrestled to the ground, rolling over and over in the dirt.

Alarmed, both dogs started barking at once, pacing and circling and managing to get wound up in each other's leashes. They didn't stop barking until they saw their two masters finally help each other up and start brushing off their clothes.

"It's OK, guys," James said, untangling the leashes. "We were just playing like you two do sometimes."

Allison removed a small twig that had implanted itself in her ponytail. "We'd better all behave now," she laughed. "Some other people are coming down the trail."

The four of them bade farewell to the chipmunks, savored one last view, and headed up the path to the parking lot as a trio of giggling Girl Scouts skipped by them.

"We need to hightail it down the mountain and get our goats settled in," said James, unlocking the truck. "Rick Moser told Dad he'd stop by our campsite near Farmer's Korner this evening to see if we need anything."

Allison pulled the door of the pickup shut after the dogs had settled in their respective spots beside her on the seat. "Hey, creep!" She turned toward her brother as he swung the truck and trailer on to Swan Mountain Road. "Thanks for stopping there. You're OK after all—for a brother."

"You're not so bad yourself—for a sister," James grinned.

Allison scratched Ribbon's furry head, looked out the side window, and squinted up at the cobalt, cloud-strewn sky. This definitely promised to be an awesome summer.

 The summer days settled into a slow, sweet rhythm. James and Allison heated their meals on the camp stove and made sure the two Border Collies kept watchful eyes on the one hundred fifty goats, as they contentedly chomped on the sea of weeds that surrounded them. Each afternoon Allison had Ribbon practice "shedding" or separating specified goats from the herd and then holding them away from the rest until signaled to return them. This skill test was the only one that had tripped Ribbon up the previous August at the sheepdog trials at the Colorado State Fair in Pueblo. Afterward, James had assured Allison that, with practice and a little more maturity, Ribbon would get the hang of this maneuver—and he had been right. By midsummer, the dog was accomplishing the task like a champ, and Allison felt more confident about their chances in Meeker in September.

Both Ribbon and Spirit happily adjusted to their daily herding chores with the goats and were especially excited when it was time to load the herd into the trailer and move to a new location around Summit County. The goats and dogs attracted considerable attention wherever they went—from residents and tourists alike. Cars often lined up along the roadside and senior citizens and young families piled out to watch the "weed whackers" through binoculars or snap pictures from a distance. Ribbon and Spirit seemed to sense whenever they were on display and would jump and run and crouch and circle the goats with added enthusiasm.

Allison, too, enjoyed photographing the goats and the dogs with her trusty camera and was delighted when the local paper, the *Summit Daily News*, published one of her close-ups of Ribbon in action. The accompanying article described the advantages of the goat herd over toxic chemicals in controlling the county's noxious weed overpopulation problem. It also asked that people not allow their own dogs anywhere near the herd—for the safety of the goats and the two Border Collies.

"I'm glad people seem to be heeding the dog warning," James said to Allison one day, pointing to a van and a truck that had just pulled up along the road near their present location in Breckenridge. "Those folks are keeping both their dogs on leashes."

"That's good. We sure don't need any trouble here." Allison shaded her eyes and returned the

friendly waves from the onlookers. "But I think it's kinda neat that our little weed control unit has become such a big attraction this summer. I never dreamed our goats and dogs would turn into such celebrities!"

The routine of their days was sometimes interrupted by visits from Rick Moser, who came to check on the goats' progress with the weeds, or from Tim or Gwen, who stopped by to replenish supplies and bring mail and news from the ranch.

"Are you two glad you signed up for this assignment?" Tim asked on one of his Meals on Wheels deliveries in late July. "Or is it getting pretty tiresome about now?"

James and Allison looked at each other. James answered first. "Well, Dad, the goats and dogs have been no trouble at all so far, and I guess, since I have to put up with my little sister anyway, I may as well get paid for it."

"Same goes for me," answered Allison quickly, sending her brother a withering look.

Tim chuckled as he sat down on a canvas lawn chair between them. "Well, if you two don't end up killing each other by the end of the summer, you'll both have a nice chunk of change to add to your college funds, plus some money left over to spend any way you want."

"I'm going to spend mine on a digital camera, I think," said Allison. "That'll make it easy to print my photos for the newspaper at school."

"That's not a bad idea," Tim said. "How about you, Son? You already have something in mind?"

"Yup," answered James, pushing his cowboy hat back on his forehead. "I plan to get a new electric guitar and some better sound equipment. My band has quite a few gigs lined up for the fall."

"Great!" Tim looked from his son to his daughter, then smiled. "I am lucky to have two such hard-working, creative, talented kids." Ribbon and Spirit, who had been sitting side by side at Tim's feet, rose up as if on cue, put their paws on his knees, and stared at him intently. "OK, OK, you silly mutts!" Tim laughed, cuffing each dog affectionately behind the ears. "I am lucky to have two such hard-working, creative, talented dogs, too."

Both dogs barked in unison. And a few loud bleats were heard from the goats chowing down nearby. "Hey, no comments from the peanut gallery!" Allison giggled, basking in the warmth of her family's camaraderie. She wished this summer could go on forever.

That night, after heating up Gwen's stick-to-the-ribs beef stew and her melt-in-your-mouth buttermilk biscuits, James and Allison decided to roast marshmallows over the dying coals to make s'mores. Ribbon and Spirit hovered close by, their noses quivering like rabbits'. "No chocolate for you two!" Allison patted their heads. "Chocolate isn't good for dogs—the veterinarian says the caffeine in it can even give you a heart attack. But, if you play your cards right, you may get a graham cracker or a marshmallow."

After their gooey dessert was consumed and the dishes washed and dried, James reached for his battered guitar and started softly strumming and humming an old cowboy song taught him a long time ago by their grandfather. Spirit leaned against his leg and appeared to be enjoying the music.

Pulling on her favorite pink hooded sweatshirt against the cool mountain night air, Allison stretched out on her back on a blanket, her hands tucked under her head, and gazed up at the spectacular starry sky. Ribbon nestled at her side and sighed contentedly.

Just then a shooting star blazed across the heavens and Allison quickly yelled to James to look up.

"Wow! That's amazing!" James watched in wonder until the shooting star disappeared from view. "It's really true the best things in life are free!"

"Yup," Allison agreed. "Rainbows, sunsets, shooting stars…." Ribbon sat up on the blanket and let out a short howl.

"And the love of a good dog," quipped James.

Allison smiled. "Yes—and the love of a good dog." Even in the darkness she could tell Ribbon was smiling too.

 By the last week in August, the nip of autumn could already be felt in the high country air, and Allison, now wearing a sweatshirt even during the day, knew she had to come to terms with the reality that summer and the adventures of their little weed patrol were quickly coming to an end. Even though she looked forward to the busy start of school and seeing friends again, she hated to say goodbye to these lazy days spent with the goats, the dogs, and her big brother.

The time had come to move the herd of goats to their final munching grounds on a flat meadow on the shores of Giberson Bay at the northwestern edge of Lake Dillon. Because the Meeker Sheepdog Trials were less than two weeks away, James suggested to Allison that they allow Ribbon to round up and load the goats all by herself without Spirit's help. Pride erupted in Allison as she watched her wonderful Border Collie, following her signals to a tee, guide every last sassy goat inside the trailer.

"I think she's definitely ready, little sister," James observed, smiling broadly. "Spirit and I had our turn at

Meeker, now it's Ribbon's and your turn. You're both gonna do great."

Allison joyously hugged her dog and then gave her brother a high-five. She felt they were ready too.

The next morning started out cool and crisp with a lovely, light mist hanging over the lake. After finishing a quick breakfast of "o.j." and cold cereal, James and Allison rinsed their bowls and cups and stowed them in the camper.

"Now that we're closer to the road, we need to be extra observant and careful with the dogs and goats, Sis," James counseled, running his hands through his unruly hair as he scanned the growing number of cars stopping along the Dillon Dam Road. "It looks like we're attracting more attention than ever."

Allison nodded, then pulled a bright turquoise baseball cap over her auburn ponytail in anticipation of the morning sun. "I want to take a picture of all those goat groupies taking pictures of us," she said, turning to kneel beside her duffel bag. It took her a few minutes to finally retrieve her camera from underneath several layers of clean socks and underwear. When she stood up, Allison sensed immediately that something was wrong.

James, with Spirit at his heels, was running through the middle of the herd of goats, waving both arms wildly in the air. An enormous, scruffy-looking, tan dog suddenly came into view, nipping at the hind leg of one panicked goat that was heading straight for the Dam Road.

Allison felt like she was glued to the ground. She couldn't think. She couldn't move. Everything seemed to be unfolding in slow motion. Then she heard her brother's frantic whistles and the piercing sound of screeching brakes. "Oh, no!" Allison gasped. "Ribbon! Where is Ribbon?"

A sob escaped from her throat as her legs finally started to move. She ran as fast as she could, stumbling once over a clump of weeds. She scrambled up and didn't stop until she saw her brother's dark head bending over something lying at the side of the road. Something black and white. Her dog. Her precious Ribbon. Tears blurred her vision as she finally reached them. James stopped stroking the Border Collie's limp body to put his arm around Allison's shoulders. "She was trying to intercept the goat when the car hit her." Her brother's voice seemed to come from a million miles away. "She's hurt, Sis, but she's still breathing."

Allison reached out and lightly patted Ribbon's ruff. She drew in her breath when she noticed that the dog's front right leg was bent at an alarming angle. "Oh,

Ribbon, I'm so sorry," she whispered into her ear. "I'm so sorry. Please be OK, girl. Please be OK." Ribbon sighed softly, but didn't open her eyes.

A police officer, carrying a large clipboard, walked over and knelt on the other side of Ribbon. "Is this your dog, Miss?" Allison looked up at him, but no sound came from her throat.

James stood up and walked around to the officer, who stood up too and began making notes on his clipboard. She could hear her brother answering the man's questions, but couldn't make out the words.

Ribbon's body suddenly shuddered. Allison laid her head gently on the dog's chest, her tears wetting the soft fur. "Keep breathing, Ribbon. Keep breathing," she whispered.

A few minutes passed before she felt James' strong arms pulling her up to a sitting position. He looked pale but in control of his emotions. "Allison, the policeman is going to take you and Ribbon to the nearest veterinary clinic over in Frisco," he said, taking his sister's face in both hands as he spoke. "I have to stay here with Spirit and the goats, but I'll call Dad and Mom on the cell phone and tell them where you are." Allison stared at her brother with a dazed look. "Sis, do you understand what

I just said?" After a few moments she nodded and slowly got to her feet.

The officer opened the back door of the patrol car as James picked up Ribbon and gently placed her in the back seat on a blanket. Allison numbly slid in beside her dog.

James closed the car door and leaned in the window. "Ribbon's going to be OK. We have to believe that." Allison, tears spilling down her cheeks, could only nod.

As the officer pulled the patrol car carefully out onto the Dillon Dam Road and headed west toward Frisco, Allison buried her head in her hands. What if Ribbon wasn't going to be OK?

 Allison jumped up from her seat in the veterinary clinic waiting room as soon as she saw her parents coming through the sliding glass door. Several minutes passed while Gwen held her tight and Tim stroked her hair. Finally Allison composed herself enough to straighten up and look into her parents' worried faces. "Ribbon is in surgery right now," she told them in a hoarse voice. "The veterinarian is trying to fix her right front leg first. He's not sure if she has a major injury to her head." Her voice trailed off, and tears welled up in her eyes as she remembered her dog's limp body lying at the side of the road.

"Oh, honey, I'm so sorry this happened," Gwen said, fishing in her purse for a tissue to dry her daughter's tears. "Let's sit down—you look exhausted."

Tim led them to a leather sofa at the far end of the waiting room. "I'm going over to check on James and see how he and Spirit are making out with the goats. I'll call over here in a little while to see if there's any more news about Ribbon." He bent down and kissed

Allison's wet cheek. "You hang in there, sweetheart. Ribbon's very strong and so are you." He squeezed her hand before he left.

Allison blew her nose on the tissue Gwen offered her, then gratefully leaned her head on her mother's shoulder. "It's all my fault, Mom. I wasn't watching Ribbon like I should have been. I knelt down to get my camera out of my duffel bag and that's when everything broke loose." She dabbed at her eyes with another tissue. "If I had been paying attention, I would have noticed that big tan dog start to chase the goat toward the road, and I could have signaled Ribbon to stay put."

Gwen gently cupped her hands under Allison's chin so she could look her directly in the eyes. "Allison, remember Ribbon is a Border Collie—her instinct is to protect the herd. Nothing could have stopped her from running to save that goat—not even you."

"But she always follows my commands, Mom. If only I'd..."

Just then, the veterinarian, Dr. Barker, a tall, husky, sandy-haired man with a surgical mask dangling around his neck, crossed the waiting room and pulled up a chair next to the sofa. After introducing himself to Gwen, he sat down and took Allison's hand in his. "I have some good news and some bad news, Allison. The good news is that Ribbon regained consciousness before we prepped her for surgery. That's a very good indication that if she does have a head injury, it's not very serious."

Listening intently, Allison didn't take her eyes off Dr. Barker. She swallowed hard and her voice quivered as she asked, "What's the bad news?"

"Well, Ribbon's right front leg was pretty badly mangled, and I had to remove part of the bone. That means even if she heals perfectly, that leg will always be shorter and weaker."

"But she's going to recover...I mean she's not going to die?" Allison looked from the vet to her mother and back to the vet.

"No, she's not going to die," Dr. Barker reassured her, patting her hand. "She'll have a permanent limp, but you'll be able to take her home in a couple of days."

Tears again ran down Allison's cheeks, but these tears were tears of joy. "May I see her?"

"Yes, come on back. I'm certain your face is the one she'll want to see when she wakes up from the anesthesia."

Gwen stood up and shook hands with the veterinarian. "Thank you so much for everything you've done for Ribbon."

"Oh, yes, thank you, Dr. Barker!" Allison exclaimed, impulsively jumping up and giving the big man a hug.

"You're very welcome. Ribbon seems like a wonderful dog."

"Oh, she absolutely is," Allison agreed as the three of them walked toward the recovery area. "She's the best Border Collie in Colorado!"

Ribbon was lying on her left side in a large, clean kennel, her right front leg bandaged and splinted with a small padded board. Her breathing was even and deep and her eyes were closed.

Allison settled herself next to her dog, being careful not to bump the injured leg. She stroked Ribbon's head and whispered in her ear, "You're going to be fine, girl. You're going to be just fine."

Gwen started to kneel beside her daughter. but stood back up when her cell phone rang and went out into the hall to get better reception. On the other end of the line Tim's voice sounded full of worry, but he gave a sigh of relief when Gwen told him the good news about Ribbon.

A few minutes later, Gwen returned to Ribbon's kennel carrying a Snickers candy bar and a bottle of water for Allison that the receptionist had given her.

"I thought you'd be pretty hungry and thirsty by now," she began then stopped in her tracks. Allison was smiling from ear to ear. With eyes wide open, Ribbon had lifted her head and she was smiling too.

 After a few days of observation at the veterinary clinic, Dr. Barker pronounced Ribbon strong enough to go home. Her leg was beginning to heal and she showed no obvious signs of a head injury. However, the vet stressed the need to watch her carefully, as sometimes complications from a concussion can show up weeks, even months later.

"My mom is a nurse, so she knows what to look for," said Allison.

"I didn't realize that," Dr. Barker replied. "Then I'm sending Ribbon home in very good hands."

Gwen blushed. "Well, I'm very used to caring for human patients, but don't assume I know everything about animals. Please give us all the usual instructions— we both need to hear them so we can do everything right for this dog."

Ribbon stayed very still as Dr. Barker showed Allison and her mother how to change the bandage and resplint the leg every day. She gently licked the vet's hand when he demonstrated how to get her to take her antibiotic pills tucked inside a liver treat. "I wish all my patients were as easy to take care of as you are, Ribbon," Dr. Barker commented as he lifted the dog down off the examining table.

Allison hooked Ribbon's leash on her collar, then gave Dr. Barker a hug. "I told you she's the best Border Collie in Colorado!" she called back over her shoulder as girl and dog disappeared out the door.

Time seemed to zoom by as Allison started her classes, attended planning meetings for the school paper, and rushed home after school every day to check on her patient. In true Ribbon fashion, the dog adapted quickly to walking on her splinted leg and even tried to keep up with Spirit in their favorite pastime of herding the family cat, Screech, an overweight gray tabby, around the house.

The date for the Meeker Sheepdog Trials came and went and Allison tried not to think about what might have been if the accident hadn't happened. But deep inside, part of her felt she had let everybody down—her parents, James, but most of all Ribbon. If only she had somehow been able to stop Ribbon from running into the path of that car, Ribbon would have had a chance to show the world that she was a true herding champion. On the other hand, another part of Allison felt that she should just be grateful that her best friend had survived and was here to come home to every day.

One afternoon James came into the kitchen, slung his backpack on the table, then noticed the sad look on his sister's face as he lowered himself into a chair across from her. "What's wrong? You look like you just lost your best friend."

Allison tried to smile. "No, I was just thinking I should be very glad I still have my best friend." She bent down to kiss the top of Ribbon's head as the dog leaned against her thigh. "But I also can't help thinking that it's all my fault that Ribbon got hurt. I should have been paying attention to her that day when the tan dog started chasing the goats and…"

"Whoa! Hold it!" James interrupted. "I was paying attention and I still wasn't able to prevent the accident from happening. I yelled and whistled at the top of my lungs, but Ribbon was on automatic pilot by then. Her instincts kicked in and she was totally focused on saving that goat—no matter what."

Allison looked intently at her brother. "That's what Mom says, too. But you both aren't telling me that just to make me feel better, are you?"

"No! Honest! I've played it over again and again in my mind." James looked down at his hands and then back at his sister. "I felt really guilty at first, too, and then I finally realized it was just one of those things that can happen. By the way, the owner of the tan dog came over to me after you and Ribbon left in the patrol car."

"He did? What did he say?"

"He apologized about his dog getting loose. He swears he had him on a leash, but the dog was so excited he broke free and took off after the goats. He felt really guilty about Ribbon getting hit by the car—just like you and I did."

Allison gently stroked Ribbon's ruff for a few moments then returned her focus to James. "I've been thinking that maybe you and I should offer to help pay for Ribbon's medical bills out of our summer earnings. I can live without a digital camera a while longer."

James nodded. "And I can live without a new guitar. We'll tell Mom and Dad tonight."

Suddenly, Screech and Spirit came careening into the kitchen from the living room, circled the table, then left the way they had come. Ribbon quickly jumped up and limped after them. "Ribbon seems to be the only one not worrying about any of this," James observed after the furry flurry had subsided. "Maybe we shouldn't underestimate your dog, Sis. Given time, she just might be able to compensate for that injured leg well enough to still be a herder. The Meeker Championship will come around again next September, you know."

Allison was afraid to get her hopes up about the possibility of Ribbon herding again, but she decided to ask Dr. Barker's opinion at Ribbon's appointment the following day. After carefully examining the incision on Ribbon's leg, the veterinarian watched Allison walk her dog in the hallway without the splint so he could evaluate her gait and balance. After a few minutes, Allison brought Ribbon back in the exam room and waited anxiously to hear what Dr. Barker had to say.

The big man easily lifted the Border Collie up on the table and placed a fresh bandage on her leg. "Well, I can say with certainty that the incision has no signs of infection," he said, looking up at Allison and her mother. "You two are obviously very good nurses. Her leg is healing just fine, and it's a good sign that she doesn't seem reluctant to bear weight on that leg. As a matter of fact, I think you can leave the splint off now and let her run outside. Just continue putting the bandage on every day to keep the incision clean."

"Do you think she'll ever be able to run fast enough to be able to herd again?" Allison swallowed and crossed her fingers under the table.

Gwen ruffled Allison's hair then turned to the veterinarian. "Allison and Ribbon were registered to participate at the Meeker Sheepdog Trials but had to withdraw because of the accident. I think she's wondering if Ribbon's injury means she'll never be able to compete at that level."

"I see," said Dr. Barker, putting his huge hands on Allison's shoulders and looking directly into her eyes. "I can't say for sure, but I don't think it's impossible. I've seen dogs who've even lost a leg be able to zoom around on their other three without any problem. We know your dog has spunk, judging from the way she's bounced back already, so she may eventually be back up to speed—literally."

A wide smile crept across Allison's face even before the vet had stopped talking. She reached up and hugged Dr. Barker and then hugged Ribbon. "See, girl, there's always next year. Give me a high five!" And Ribbon did just that.

On the way home to the ranch, Allison's heart felt light for the first time since the dreadful dark day of Ribbon's accident. Not only did she still have her precious pet beside her, but maybe, just maybe, they would have their chance to show their stuff at Meeker after all.

 The last two weeks of September in the Rocky Mountains were Allison's favorite time of the entire year. She loved the brilliant blue of the Colorado sky, the glittering gold of the changing aspen leaves, and the delicious chill of the autumn air.

Anxious to be outside during her favorite season, she rushed home from school, quickly emptied her backpack on the kitchen table, and changed from her school clothes into a pair of worn jeans and a long-sleeved orange tee shirt that sported the message: "If you're lucky enough to live in the mountains, you're lucky enough!" After preparing two peanut butter and jelly sandwiches, she wrapped them in a napkin and put them in her backpack along with a bottle of water, a plastic bowl, a thermos of lemonade, a tattered blanket, and her trusty camera. Ribbon waited expectantly by the door while Allison took time to write a quick note for her mother to let her know where they were going.

Finally they both burst outside into the afternoon sunshine and headed up a hill behind the house. Allison observed Ribbon carefully as the dog scampered ahead. Her right front leg was noticeably shorter than the left and it bowed outward, but the Border Collie didn't seem to care. "Dogs are much more adaptable than people," Allison's father always liked to say. Now she knew exactly what he meant. Ribbon was obviously enjoying every minute with no thought to her new handicap.

When they reached their favorite shady spot under a grove of aspen trees, Allison spread out the blanket on the grass and plopped down on her back to gaze up at the sky. Ribbon came and sat next to her, but didn't settle in. She nudged the backpack several times with her long Collie nose until Allison gave in and sat up. "OK, OK, you hungry critter," Allison laughed, bringing out the sandwiches. "We'll have our picnic right away." She broke off a large corner of one sandwich for the dog, who gulped it down immediately and then stared intently at Allison until she gave her more. Soon both sandwiches were completely gone—except for a purple smear of grape jelly at the side of Ribbon's mouth. In an instant that too disappeared when the Border Collie licked her chops. To wash down their snack, Allison poured water into the plastic bowl for Ribbon, then took a long, satisfying swallow of icy lemonade from her thermos.

A gentle breeze that rustled the aspens overhead caused them both to look skyward. Suddenly, a delicate golden leaf floated down from above and landed smack in the middle of Ribbon's forehead. "Stay real still, girl," Allison said, scrambling for her camera to capture this trademark moment. Ribbon drew up the corners of her mouth in her signature smile and looked straight into the camera lens as Allison snapped the picture. "You're such a ham—that should turn out great!"

Rolling over on her back, Allison pulled the dog to her side. She could feel the warmth of Ribbon's furry body next to hers, and she shuddered when she thought back to how close she had come to losing her. The Border Collie sighed contentedly and snuggled closer while Allison gazed up through the graceful white branches of the aspen trees. "Thank you, God, for giving me back my dog."

Soon Ribbon was snoring softly, and while she slept Allison shot several photos from different angles up through the canopy of yellow leaves above them, a technique she had once seen used on a Colorado postcard. "We're so lucky to live here," she thought to herself, remembering her dear grandmother's stories of life on this ranch many years ago. Although it was a tough grind of unending hard work, Grandma said she always

RIBBON THE BORDER COLLIE

knew God had eventually put her in exactly the right spot. Brought here from the Midwest as a young bride, she had instantly fallen in love with the serenity and splendor of the Rocky Mountains. "If I'd never seen the blue sky and gold leaves of a Colorado autumn, I'd be a much poorer woman," Allison had heard her say many times. She knew just what her grandmother had been talking about—it was what singer John Denver had called "Rocky Mountain High."

A low, rumbling sound interrupted Allison's thoughts and she sat up on the blanket, waking Ribbon at her side. Looking down the hill toward the barn, she saw her father's pickup truck come to a stop. "Wow! It must be getting late, girl," she said, standing up and brushing herself off. Ribbon stretched and stepped off the blanket while Allison gathered all her things together and put them in the backpack. "I'll race you to the house!"

They were heading down the hill, with Ribbon way in the lead, when the bandage on the dog's leg came undone and started unfurling behind her. Allison yelled at Ribbon to stop, but the Border Collie kept on going. Then Allison tried whistling the halt signal that usually stopped Ribbon in her tracks, but, instead of stopping, the dog continued in the direction of the house.

Allison was out of breath by the time she reached the truck where her father was unloading bales of hay. "What's going on, honey?" Tim asked, straightening up and rubbing his back with both hands.

Allison took a minute to catch her breath before answering. "As we were coming down the hill, Ribbon's bandage started coming off, so I yelled and then I whistled for her to stop, but it was like she didn't even hear me. She just kept on going."

"That's not like her," Tim commented, shaking his head.

Just then Ribbon came down off the back porch and trotted in their direction. The bandage was nowhere to be seen.

"Oh, Daddy, what if..."

"What if what?" Her father turned and saw Allison's stricken face.

"What if Ribbon can't hear?"

Chapter 10

Dr. Barker confirmed Allison's fears the next day. Although Ribbon had no trouble hearing if she was right by your side, the hearing in her right ear was quite diminished, making it difficult for her to hear if she was any distance away.

After finishing his exam, Dr. Barker said, "Remember, she was struck by the car on the right side of her body. I'm sure that's the explanation for the hearing loss on that side. None of us picked up on it earlier because she wasn't allowed outside to run until recently."

Allison struggled to control her emotions. She knew this news meant that Ribbon's herding days were now definitely over. A Border Collie with an injured leg might be able to compensate, but not a Border Collie who couldn't hear her owner's signals.

As soon as Allison, Gwen, and Ribbon climbed into the pickup in the veterinary clinic parking lot, Allison let the tears come. She buried her face in Ribbon's thick ruff and began to sob. Gwen didn't start the truck and sat quietly stroking her daughter's tangled hair. Ribbon waited patiently until Allison's sobs finally subsided, then reached her warm, pink tongue around to lick the girl's wet cheeks. "That tickles, you silly dog!" Allison giggled in spite of herself, kissing Ribbon on the top of her head and accepting a tissue from Gwen.

"You'll probably feel a lot better now after having a good cry," Gwen said, turning the key in the ignition and backing out of the parking space. "I know the past few weeks have been an emotional roller coaster for you, honey."

Allison nodded in agreement, straightening around in her seat and fastening her seatbelt. "It just seems so unfair that Ribbon won't be able to do what she was born to do."

Gwen glanced over at her daughter and Ribbon nestled side by side on the seat and then smiled as she returned her gaze to the busy highway. "Well, I think at this very moment Ribbon is actually doing two things she was born to do."

"What do you mean?"

"She's watching over you and also being your best friend." Gwen paused, wanting to choose her words carefully. "I know your dad and other ranchers always say Border Collies are working dogs, born to herd, and they're probably right about that, but that doesn't mean there's not a lot of other things they're good at, too."

Allison stroked Ribbon's chest with both hands and pondered what her mother had said. They drove the rest of the way to the ranch in silence.

As soon as they entered the kitchen, Gwen went directly to the refrigerator door and took a small scrap of paper from under a cow-shaped magnet advertising a Silverthorne feed store. "I remembered this newspaper clipping on our way home. I've had it on the frig for years because it's advice I always want to remember."

Allison took the piece of paper from her mother and sat down at the table. "I've noticed this before, but never really paid any attention to it."

"Well, it might mean something to you right now," Gwen said. "It was written by a very wise lady named Erma Bombeck. She died a few years ago, but I always loved reading her newspaper column and hearing her philosophy of life."

Allison read out loud: "When I stand before God at the end of my life, I would hope that I would not have a single bit of talent left and could say, 'I used everything you gave me.'" Allison handed the slip of paper back to Gwen. "I get it—you think it will make me feel better if I realize that Ribbon has talents she hasn't even used yet."

"Exactly!" her mother replied. "We just have to find out what those talents are and give her a way to discover another purpose in life." Allison seemed lost in thought until the sound of Ribbon's tail thumping loudly on the kitchen floor brought her focus back to the conversation. "Well, what do you think, honey?" Gwen asked. "Are you game for finding something new for Ribbon to work on?"

"Yes, definitely!" Allison answered. "What do you think, girl?"

Ribbon's shaggy head popped up above the edge of the table. Her smile was her answer.

 As the last of the aspen leaves fluttered to the ground and the first snow of the season dusted the mountain peaks, Allison stayed busy with all the activities of the fall season. She took pictures for the school paper at the Harvest Bazaar and then turned her attention to making a costume for the church's annual Spookarama Halloween Party. She decided to be Dorothy from the Wizard of Oz and take Ribbon along as Toto. When she tried to convince James to dress up as the Tin Man, he immediately and flatly refused, stating he was much too old for such things, and, anyway, his band was scheduled to play for the High School Halloween Dance.

Tim and Gwen, however, willingly dressed up as the farm couple with the pitchfork in *American Gothic* and accompanied Dorothy and Toto to the church basement for the Halloween festivities. Allison's long-time pal Charley, whose real name was Charlotte (which she hated), greeted them at the door. She was dressed as Ronald McDonald and was passing out hamburgers. Because her own hair was fire engine red and curly, she didn't need a wig.

As the evening wore on, everyone, even Ribbon, participated in the games and seemed to be having a good time. The Border Collie was constantly surrounded by a ring of young kids who jostled for turns hugging and petting her. Through it all, she remained amazingly calm and patient, even when an exuberant two-year-old suddenly climbed on her back and held onto her ears. From across the room Gwen watched her daughter gently but firmly pull the toddler off the dog and show him how to softly pet Ribbon's ruff. At that moment an idea popped into Gwen's head.

On their way back home from the party, Gwen couldn't wait any longer to share her brainstorm. "Allison and Ribbon, listen up," she said, turning toward them in the back seat of the car. "I was very impressed with how well both of you handled yourselves in the noise and chaos of the party tonight, and watching you gave me what I think is a great idea for a future job for Ribbon."

Allison leaned forward and rested her chin on the back of the front seat. Her dog followed suit, her ears standing at attention. "We're all ears," laughed Allison. "Hurry up and tell us your idea."

Gwen gave them both an affectionate pat on the head. "I think you should train Ribbon to be a therapy dog."

"What is a therapy dog, Mom?"

"A therapy dog is trained to visit patients in hospitals, nursing homes, and rehab centers. As you well know, animals have a special way of making people feel better. I remember when I worked on a children's cancer unit in Denver—before you were born—there was a Golden Retriever named Hope who visited one day a week. Sometimes…" Gwen paused for a minute, remembering, then continued. "Sometimes Hope was the only one who was able to get the kids to smile and forget they were sick."

Tim, who had been listening quietly to the conversation, turned the car into their lane. "I can recall you talking about that therapy dog back then, Gwen. As a matter of fact, it seemed like the dog made as big an impression on the nurses as she did on the patients."

Gwen nodded in the darkness. "We used to look forward to that big, furry bundle of love walking down the hall with her owner. We just knew it was going to be a better day for everyone. Animals by their nature always live in the present moment—not wasting time regretting the past or worrying about the future like we humans do—and being around them helps us stay in the moment too."

Allison and Ribbon had been hanging on every word. Now they both hung their heads farther over the seat. "How do we make Ribbon into a therapy dog, Mom?"

"Well, Dorothy and Toto," Gwen laughed, giving each of them another playful pat on the head, "give me a day or two to do some research and ask around at the hospital, and I'll find out about all the requirements for you, OK?"

After he stopped the car next to the house, Tim turned to look at his daughter. "You know, Allison, I always say Border Collies are bred to herd, and that's a fact. But there's another fact I know about them, too."

"What's that?"

"Unlike some other breeds of dogs, Border Collies love to learn new things throughout their lives," Tim answered. "That means Ribbon should have no trouble at all learning to be a therapy dog."

"I'm not worried at all about her learning ability, Dad. I think she'll be terrific with patients." Allison gave her dog a quick squeeze. "After all, she makes me smile every day, don't you, girl?"

Ribbon let out a loud bark in agreement and had everyone in the car smiling.

Chapter 12

Every year Allison would get excited as the Thanksgiving and Christmas holidays grew near—she loved all the shopping and baking and decorating—but this year was different. "I wish Christmas was already over," Allison announced, placing one of Gwen's freshly-baked pumpkin pies in the top of a bulging picnic basket and carefully hooking the lid.

Gwen put down her wooden mixing spoon and stared at her daughter. "Why in the world would you say that?"

"I guess I'm just much more excited about Ribbon's Pet Partner evaluation than I am about the holidays," Allison explained.

"Now I get it," Gwen smiled. "I'm excited, too." Her research on therapy dogs had led her to the Delta Society website where she found exactly what she was looking for. The Delta Society's Pet Partners Program was described as "a service program that trains and certifies people-animal volunteer teams to visit health care settings." She immediately ordered the home study manual for Allison and Ribbon and signed them up for an evaluation session in Denver during the first week of the new year.

The oven timer signaled that the last pumpkin pie was ready to come out. Gwen set the fragrant pie on the counter to cool and took off her apron. "We don't have time to think about all that now. Our mission at the moment is to make our own private Meals on Wheels delivery to the O'Briens, and if we don't get this food over to them soon, they will miss out on Thanksgiving dinner altogether."

"Can Ribbon go with us to deliver the food?" asked Allison. "The Pet Partners home study manual says she needs to learn to be around food without grabbing for it. And also she needs to get comfortable being around people with canes and walkers. Mrs. O'Brien uses a walker, remember?"

"Yes, you're right, she does. OK, come on, Ribbon. This visit to the O'Briens can be part of your training program." Gwen laughed when she realized the dog was already waiting for them at the door.

Mr. O'Brien, a thin, stooped man in flannel shirt and overalls, ushered them into the dimly-lit living room of the old frame farmhouse. His rosy-cheeked, white-haired wife sat in a recliner, her knitting in her lap. A delighted smile spread across her broad face as Ribbon trotted over and sat at her feet. "Well, who is this pretty thing?" the old woman cooed, reaching down to stroke the Border Collie's shiny fur. "Ain't you a beauty!"

"This is my dog, Ribbon," Allison said, kneeling beside Mrs. O'Brien. "She's going to be a therapy dog and visit patients in hospitals and nursing homes—once she passes her evaluation."

Ribbon held up her right paw and Mrs. O'Brien reached out and gave her a vigorous handshake. "Well, Ribbon, I think you'll help those patients more than any old pills ever would."

Ribbon let out a loud bark and everyone laughed.

"I'll help you to the kitchen, dear," Mr. O'Brien said, as he positioned her walker in front of her chair. "You won't believe the wonderful Thanksgiving dinner these good neighbors have brought us."

Allison, with Ribbon at her heels, went ahead into the kitchen to help Gwen unpack the picnic basket. By the time the O'Briens entered the room, all the fixings of a turkey dinner were laid out on the wooden table.

"My! My! Everything looks absolutely delicious!" Mrs. O'Brien exclaimed, easing herself into her favorite kitchen chair. "Won't you folks stay and eat with us?"

"I wish we could, but I have dinner on the stove at home," answered Gwen. "My husband and son will be as hungry as wolves after they finish their morning chores. But we'll come back tomorrow to collect the dishes and maybe have a piece of pie with you."

"Mom's pumpkin pie is the world's best!" interjected Allison.

Mrs. O'Brien gave both Allison and Ribbon a lingering hug. "Thank you so much for making our holiday so special. And be sure to bring my Ribbon with you when you come back."

"We will," Allison called out as they headed out the door.

Mr. O'Brien followed them to the car and shook hands awkwardly with Allison and Gwen, and then with Ribbon's raised paw. "Thank you so much for coming today. I haven't seen my wife this happy in a very long time."

As they drove away, Allison looked down at Ribbon on the seat beside her and then over at her mother. "I don't think Ribbon is going to have any trouble passing her therapy dog evaluation, do you?"

"Absolutely not," Gwen agreed. "She completely charmed Mrs. O'Brien. Ribbon's a natural, aren't you, girl?"

Ribbon just stretched out on the seat and let out a long, doggy sigh.

A light, powdery snow began falling on Christmas Eve afternoon as Gwen, Allison, and Ribbon made their next meal delivery to the O'Brien farm. Laden down with a baked ham, scalloped potatoes, and a large tin of flaky star-shaped sugar cookies, they gratefully entered the warm kitchen when Mr. O'Brien opened the door.

Mrs. O'Brien, who was seated at the table with a gaily-wrapped package in her lap, held out both arms as Ribbon greeted her with a sloppy kiss. "Merry Christmas, you lovely dog!" she exclaimed. "Merry Christmas to all of you. Sit down and have some hot cider to warm your insides. Papa just made some for us—it has a cinnamon stick in it."

Allison helped Mr. O'Brien fill four mugs with the steaming cider, passed one each to her mother and Mrs. O'Brien, then sat down and cradled the warm cup in her cold hands.

Mrs. O'Brien was petting Ribbon and smiling like a Cheshire cat.

"Well, go on, Mama," Mr. O'Brien said, beaming at his wife. "Show them what you have there."

The old woman placed the wrapped package on the floor in front of the Border Collie. "This is for you, Ribbon," she said proudly. "I just hope it fits."

As Ribbon started to paw at the wrapping paper, Allison joined her on the floor and helped unfasten the tape. "It's a sweater!" she cried, holding up the knitted, dark green creation for her mother to see. "Ribbon, you'll look beautiful!"

The dog sat patiently as Allison and Mrs. O'Brien pulled the sweater over her shaggy head and pushed her front paws through the two sleeves.

"Why, I actually think you're smiling," exclaimed Mrs. O'Brien, looking down at Ribbon and clapping her hands in delight. "I wanted you to have something warm to wear to your therapy rounds."

"That was so thoughtful of you," Gwen said. "Ribbon will wear it proudly."

"Your family has been so good to us," Mr. O'Brien said quietly. "We never seem to have any way to repay you." He put his mug down and looked fondly at his wife. "But Mama got this idea of a sweater for Ribbon Thanksgiving night, and she's been knitting up a storm ever since."

"Well, we—I mean Ribbon—has something for you, too." Allison dug in the pocket of her parka and brought out a rectangular present wrapped in gold foil. "Here, girl, you do the honors." The Border Collie carefully took the package in her mouth and carried it to Mrs. O'Brien.

The old woman wasted no time unwrapping the photograph in its slender gold frame. Grinning from ear to ear, she held the picture up for her husband to see. "Look, it's my precious Ribbon with an aspen leaf on her forehead, and she's actually smiling! I'll keep it on the coffee table right next to my recliner so I can look at it all the time." She bent down and hugged Ribbon so enthusiastically she almost knocked the dog off her feet. "What a wonderful gift and what a wonderful dog!"

For the next few minutes Ribbon sat patiently by Mrs. O'Brien's chair while everyone finished their cider, then she offered her paw for the old woman to shake. "Merry Christmas, Ribbon!" Mrs. O'Brien said. "Thank you all for coming."

The snow was coming down fast as they headed for home. "It's going to be a white Christmas!" Allison clapped her mittened hands together. "Dad is going to be so pleased!"

"Why is that?" Gwen asked, looking puzzled.

"You'll find out tonight when we open our presents," Allison answered mysteriously. "Ribbon isn't the only one getting an awesome present this Christmas."

Chapter 14

Supper was over. The dishes were done. The Christmas tree in the living room was aglow with tiny red lights. An inviting fire was ablaze in the fireplace. At last the time had come to open gifts at the Colby ranch.

Tim handed Allison and James their presents first.

"This is awesome!" cried Allison, as she unwrapped a digital camera.

"Wow!" whooped James. "This is the exact guitar I've been wanting!"

"Well, you two definitely deserve these gifts," smiled Tim, sitting down on the sofa next to Gwen. "Both of you did a great job with the goats this summer. Your mother and I are very proud of your work ethic." Ribbon and Spirit sauntered into the room at that moment and settled at Tim's feet. "OK, we're proud of your work ethic, too, you mangy mutts," Tim chuckled, scratching both dogs behind their ears.

After Gwen had given both dogs their new rawhide toys from beneath the tree, she gave each of her children a kiss on the cheek before sitting back down. "Since you offered your spending money to help with Ribbon's medical bills, we wanted you both to still get what you really wanted."

Allison handed Gwen a silver and red wrapped present topped with a large plaid bow. "I hope this is something you really want, Mom."

Gwen gave the thumbs up sign after she unwrapped the book, "The Complete Works of Erma Bombeck." "Oh, honey! How thoughtful of you! You know how much I love her. I can't wait to read it!"

It was Tim's turn to open a present, and his eyes lit up when he saw the sheepskin coat Gwen had ordered for him from a western clothing catalog. "This will keep me nice and warm out on the range—thank you," he said, giving his wife a peck on the forehead.

Eventually all the presents under the tree had been opened except for a catnip mouse for Screech, who was currently taking a catnap in front of the fireplace. Gwen knelt down to gather the torn wrappings and ribbons into a pile, but Tim caught both her hands and pulled her to a standing position. "That can wait until later, my lady. There's still one more gift and it has your name on it." Allison and James exchanged knowing glances. "James and I will go outside and get it. You and Allison make a thermos of hot chocolate, gather up some blankets, and wait for us at the kitchen door."

"Aye, aye, sir," Gwen saluted as the males disappeared out the door into the cold night. Turning toward her daughter, she said, "What in the world is going on?"

"All I can say is you're going to be blown away by this present," Allison told her, giving Gwen a quick hug. After they went into the kitchen to prepare the hot chocolate, Allison decided to fill a paper bag with sugar cookies to take along as well. She was so happy and excited she couldn't help smiling from ear to ear. "This will definitely be a Christmas to remember, Mom. I guarantee it."

Shaking her head in puzzlement, Gwen put on her parka and boots and, following Tim's orders, gathered a pile of blankets including a dog-sized afghan for Spirit, while Allison put Ribbon's new green sweater on her.

Soon the door opened and Tim poked his ski-cap-covered head inside. "Your chariot awaits," he announced, grinning, as Gwen and Allison and the dogs trooped past him into the frosty air.

The snow had stopped earlier in the evening, leaving just the perfect amount of the white stuff under the rungs of the beautiful sleigh that stood before them. "Oh, my heavens!" cried Gwen as the scene before her finally sunk in. "This is Grandpa and Grandma's old sleigh that I've always loved. You've brought it back to life!"

"Yep," replied Tim, helping Gwen into the sleigh's front seat and handing her a heavy plaid wool blanket. "James and I have been working on it over at Jed's shop all fall. Now we just have to see if this old horse knows how to pull this thing." He adjusted Betsy's harness and crawled in beside Gwen as Allison and James and the two dogs settled under their blankets in the back seat.

Gwen reached over and gave both her husband and son a heartfelt "thank you" hug. "Allison was right. She said I'd be blown away by this present, and I truly am. This is the best Christmas ever." She wiped tears from her eyes with her gloves.

"Everybody ready? Here we go!" Tim snapped the reins and the startled horse got off to a jerky start, the bells on her harness jingling furiously; but within a minute or two she had settled into a steady pace and the sleigh skimmed smoothly over the fresh snow.

A full moon shone amidst a million glittering stars, casting a magical glow on the snow-capped peaks in the distance. As she snuggled down under the blankets next to her brother and their two joyful dogs, Allison had the delicious feeling that she was living right inside an

old-fashioned Christmas card scene. She considered it the icing on the cake when her parents broke into a rousing chorus of "Jingle Bells."

After a few looping circles of the back meadow, the temperature seemed to be dropping by the minute. Soon, Tim directed Betsy to head for home. As the sleigh cut through the crust of the snow-covered fields, Ribbon crawled into Allison's lap and leaned her head against her chest. "Merry Christmas!" Allison whispered in Ribbon's good ear. "We're going to start on a new adventure in the new year. Are you ready, girl?"

The dog reached up and rubbed her cold nose against Allison's cold nose. "I'll take that as a yes." Allison laughed, then she joined her father, mother, and brother in one last chorus of "Jingle Bells," as the twinkling white Christmas lights strung along the eaves of the ranch house welcomed them home.

Chapter 15

Except for a day of skiing in Vail with Charley and her family, Allison spent every minute of Christmas vacation working with Ribbon on the exercises in the Pet Partner home study manual. Now the day of Ribbon's therapy dog evaluation had arrived. A combination of excitement and nervousness made Allison turn down her mother's offer of blueberry pancakes for breakfast. Instead, she settled for a piece of buttered cinnamon toast that she surreptitiously shared with Ribbon, whose appetite was as good as usual.

During the hour-long drive down from the mountains to Denver, Allison started to worry whether this was the right thing for her Border Collie to be doing. Would Ribbon pass all the tests today? Would she even enjoy this new "career"?

"A penny for your thoughts, honey," Gwen said, looking over at her unusually quiet daughter. "You seem a little preoccupied this morning."

Allison fidgeted with the zipper of her sky blue parka. "I guess I am a little nervous. What if this isn't the right thing for Ribbon to be doing? I mean, what if she's not cut out to be a therapy dog?"

"Well," Gwen said, concentrating on the growing line of traffic as they neared the city. "That's what today's evaluation is designed to tell us. But when I think back to Ribbon's very first visit with Mrs. O'Brien, there definitely was an instant connection between them. I truly feel Ribbon is perfectly suited for this kind of work. She has a wonderful way of making everyone feel special."

Allison went back over Ribbon's and Mrs. O'Brien's interaction in her mind and had to admit her mother was right. She sighed and felt some of the tenseness in her body begin to ease. "You're right. I am forgetting what I know to be absolutely true," she said, looking down at her dog snoozing peacefully on the seat beside her. "Never underestimate the power of a Border Collie—especially this Border Collie."

True to form, Ribbon passed all of her tests with amazing ease and seemed to enjoy every minute of it. At least in the eyes of Allison and her mother, she clearly outshone all the other dogs being evaluated that day— two Golden Retrievers, a giant Saint Bernard, and one very feisty Miniature Schnauzer. She easily focused on the tasks at hand as Allison led her through her paces. She was not distracted by loud noises or strange medical equipment or even the four yellow tennis balls attached to the legs of a walker that someone pushed right by her.

When they had finished all the required tests, Mrs. Ohlson, the head Pet Partner evaluator, told Allison she was extremely impressed by how well she and Ribbon worked together as a team. "You and Ribbon are going to make a lot of people very happy. I feel it in my bones."

At the mention of bones, Ribbon let out a loud bark. Mrs. Ohlson chuckled as she knelt down and patted the dog's head. "You're right. You deserve a reward for all your good work today." She stood up and led Allison and Ribbon to a metal table strewn with bags of rawhide chew treats. She opened a bag, giving a treat to the waiting dog, then took Allison by the hand. "Now come over here and we'll fit Ribbon with her official Delta Society vest."

Allison helped the evaluator fasten the dark green vest around Ribbon's furry belly. "Let her wear this vest only when she's performing her therapy dog duties," Mrs. Ohlson cautioned. "That way, whenever you put it on her, she'll know it's time for her to go to work. We'll be sending you her official ID name tag as soon as all the paper work is processed."

Allison and Ribbon were all smiles as they crossed the room into Gwen's waiting arms. "You two made an awesome team out there!" Gwen crowed, hugging them close. "I knew you'd pass with flying colors."

On the way home, they celebrated by stopping at McDonald's to order burgers, fries, and milkshakes. At the drive-through window, the clerk noticed Ribbon's head through the car's windshield and slipped four Milkbones into a separate bag to add to their order.

As they headed into the mountains on busy Interstate 70, Gwen noticed that Allison devoured her food in record time, while Ribbon contentedly finished off all four of her Milkbones. "It looks like your appetite has returned," Gwen kidded her daughter.

"Uh, huh." Allison popped the last golden fry into her mouth and wiped a smear of ketchup from her chin with a napkin. "I'm glad Ribbon was given her own food because I was too hungry to share."

They rode in silence the rest of the way home, captivated by the brilliant crimson and orange sunset that splashed across the western sky. Ribbon, tuckered out from her long day, soon was in doggy dreamland, her upper lip quivering from time to time. Allison tenderly stroked her dog's crooked front leg and sent up a silent thank you to heaven that her best friend was still by her side.

Chapter 16

Allison awoke earlier than usual for a Saturday, a sense of anticipation flooding her whole body. Today was Ribbon's first day as an official therapy dog and Allison couldn't wait to get started.

First, she poured some beef broth over Ribbon's bowl of dry food to give her extra nutrients and energy for her big day. While the dog inhaled breakfast, Allison gathered two faded beach towels, doggy shampoo, and a stiff brush, and carried them into the bathroom. She then filled the bathtub with a few inches of warm water and attached a long rubber hose to the faucet.

Getting no response when she called Ribbon's name, Allison found her dog hiding in the laundry room, wedged under a utility shelf. "Come on, girl," Allison pleaded, kneeling beside her on the floor. "I know you don't like getting a bath, but you can't go to the nursing home today unless you have one. That's the rule."

Eventually, Ribbon crept out from beneath the shelf, and, head hung low, slowly followed Allison into the bathroom. Allison closed the door, turned the overhead heat lamp on for added warmth, and lifted the reluctant Border Collie into the tub. After wetting Ribbon's thick fur, she poured a small amount of shampoo into her palm and began sudsing the dog from head to tail. During the whole procedure, Ribbon refused to make eye contact, but she did cooperate by sitting still. Working as fast as she could, Allison used the rubber hose to rinse every bit of soap from Ribbon's fur, then lifted her out of the tub. Before she could turn and grab one of the beach towels, Ribbon started to shake her sopping wet body like the agitator in a washing machine, sending a fine spray of water all over Allison and everything else in the tiny bathroom. "You rat!" Allison cried, finally managing to tackle the dog with a towel and make her stay put. After rubbing her vigorously with both towels, Allison finished the drying process with a hairdryer. "It's cold outside, so we need to get you completely dry," Allison told her. Although Ribbon didn't like the raspy noise of the hairdryer, she did like the nice warm air it produced and grudgingly sat quietly for the rest of the ordeal. With smooth strokes, Allison brushed Ribbon's black and white coat until it glistened. Finally, she tugged Mrs. O'Brien's dark green knit sweater over Ribbon's head and gave her a kiss.

"There, now you look gorgeous!" Allison proclaimed. "But I'm totally exhausted!"

As soon as Allison unlatched the bathroom door, Ribbon made her escape, glad to be free at last. Dog and girl reached the kitchen just as Gwen came through the door, carrying two paper sacks of groceries. "Are you two almost ready for the debut of Ribbon the Therapy Dog?" Gwen asked.

"As ready as we'll ever be," answered Allison, taking one bag from her mother's arms. She started putting cans away in the cupboard. "We just finished Ribbon's bath—which was a struggle as usual."

Gwen stooped down and petted the dog's gleaming fur, then returned to her groceries. "The only one I know who hated taking baths more than Ribbon does was James when he was a toddler. It used to be World War III around here. Dad and I used to have to literally wrestle him into the tub."

"Hey, I heard that!" James commented as he loped down the stairs and joined them in the kitchen. He took Ribbon's head in both hands and gazed into her chocolate brown eyes. "Are these mean women making you bathe and wear this silly sweater?"

Allison swatted her brother playfully on the top of the head with a dishtowel. "Please don't interfere, brother dear. Today, Ribbon becomes an official therapy dog and she has to look—and smell—her best."

"Oh, that's right. Today's her first day," he said, straightening up his lanky body. "Well, sweater or no sweater, she's going to knock 'em dead."

Gwen winced. "That's not the best phrase to use about a nursing home, Son."

"Guess not." James blushed. "Well, my work here is done. I will see you ladies later."

After Gwen and Allison finished putting away the groceries, they both pulled on their coats, boots, and warm hats, ready to brave the January cold. Allison opened the back door and announced with a flourish, "It's show time!" She bowed as the spanking clean star of the day bounded past her and out into the frigid mountain air.

Chapter 17

News of Ribbon's arrival spread quickly through the halls of High Country Manor.

"Ribbon is our very first therapy dog, and everyone's very excited to meet her," Amy Madison, the pretty brunette head nurse, told Allison and her mother as they hung their coats on hooks in the reception area. "I think she'll be just what we need around here to cheer everybody up. January always brings the post-holiday blahs to the patients and the staff."

Allison removed Ribbon's green sweater and replaced it with her green Delta Society vest. "OK, now it's time to go to work. Are you ready, girl?"

Ribbon responded with a bark and a smile.

Halfway down a long corridor, Amy ushered them into a wallpapered room with a large picture window looking out on a snowy courtyard. In a neatly-made hospital bed, propped up on several pillows, was a frail, elf-like woman in a pink flannel nightgown and matching robe. Her sparse white hair was pulled back in a bun, and she had a sweet but lopsided smile.

Amy placed her hand gently on the old woman's shoulder. "This is Cora Logan, one of our favorite residents. Cora, this is Allison, her mother Gwen, and this is the dog I've been telling you about. Her name is Ribbon."

At the mention of her name, Ribbon stood up on her hind legs and reached both front paws through the metal bars of the bed's siderails. A look of sheer delight spread across Cora's wrinkled face. "Oh, my! Aren't you something?" she exclaimed, reaching her left hand across her chest to scratch behind Ribbon's ear. "Such a pretty baby."

After a minute or two, Allison noticed with alarm that Ribbon had started to lick Cora's right hand, which was tightly closed in a fist. Amy saw Allison's reaction and immediately said to Cora, "Does Ribbon's licking bother your hand, Cora?"

Cora giggled like a little girl. "Oh my no! That is the best that hand has felt since I had my stroke. Her tongue is so warm and comforting."

Ribbon kept up her gentle licking for another few minutes until Amy signaled it was time to leave. Allison tugged on Ribbon's leash, and the dog quietly got down from the bed.

"Cora, we don't want to wear you out, so we're going to go on to the next resident now," Amy said, tucking the sheets in around her and smoothing her hair.

"Thank you so much for coming, all of you," she answered. "When will you be back? I can't wait until my next massage."

Allison looked at her mother. "Next Saturday, right, Mom?"

"Yes, next Saturday, if that works with your schedule here."

Amy nodded agreement. "How does that sound to you, Cora?"

"Ribbon could come every day—if it was up to me," Cora replied, again giggling her little girl giggle.

Their next stop was in the sunny TV room at the end of the hall, where Bob Jensen, a heavyset bald man with a round face and ruddy complexion, was shuffling along behind a walker. Amy introduced everyone, then led them to a round table near the window. She excused herself when a nurse's aide, wearing a peach-colored top and white pants, beckoned to her from the doorway.

"What a dandy-looking dog," Bob said, lowering himself slowly into a cushioned chair and setting his walker to the side. "I had a cattle dog about that size when I had my ranch."

"We live on a ranch and Ribbon used to be one of our herding dogs," Allison explained. "But she had to give up herding after she was hit by a car." Ribbon approached the elderly man and put her right front leg on his lap. "She's showing you her injured leg. A car hit her leg and also the right side of her head. She lost the hearing in her right ear, so that's the main reason she can't herd anymore. Her leg is crooked, but she gets around on it really well."

Bob stroked Ribbon's offered leg and peered down at the dog over his wire-rimmed glasses. "I can see you're a real trooper there. I've got a bum leg, too, you know. Got it when I was thrown from a horse years ago. That ended my rodeo days. Arthritis has made things worse as I've gotten older, but we gotta keep moving, don't we, girl?"

They all laughed when Ribbon barked in agreement.

A few minutes later, Amy returned to take them to the auditorium where a stretching class was in progress. "Word about Ribbon has gotten out, and the residents in the exercise class insist you all stop by before you leave today."

A half dozen white-haired women in pastel jogging suits sat in a semi-circle of straight-backed chairs in front of a young blonde recreational therapist, who was enthusiastically calling out arm movements to a Broadway show tune. As the song ended, the instructor pointed to the back of the room and all heads turned in that direction. Squeals of delight broke out when Allison brought the four-legged guest of honor to the front of the room. Without any prompting, Ribbon made her way from woman to woman, shaking hands with each one before going on to the next.

Allison and her mother could still hear the excited chatter and laughter of the women behind them when they exited through the nursing home's front door. After quickly unhooking Ribbon's leash from her collar, removing her Delta Society vest, and putting on her sweater, Allison raced with her dog across the parking lot. By the time Gwen caught up, she found the two of them joyously rolling around in a snowbank. "Hey, what are you two doing?" she asked breathlessly.

"We're celebrating Ribbon's success as a therapy dog by making snow angels," Allison laughed, lying on her back and flapping her arms in the snow. Ribbon imitated her actions by awkwardly flailing from side to side next to her.

After a few minutes, Gwen unlocked the car and turned on its heater while Allison brushed the snow from Ribbon's fur and sweater and her own coat and jeans. Before long the inside of the car grew nice and toasty and they headed for home.

James and Spirit heard the car pull up and met them at the door. "How'd it go? Was Ribbon a natural? Did everyone like her sweater?" He reached out and patted Ribbon's head when she passed by.

Gwen hung up her coat and sat down at the kitchen table, as her son folded his lanky teenage body into a chair across from her. "Your sister and her dog were absolutely amazing today. They would have made Erma Bombeck very proud." She winked at her daughter as Allison came to stand beside her.

"Erma who?" James asked, looking puzzled.

"Bombeck," Allison answered. "We'll tell you about her someday when you're mature enough to understand." With that, she stuck out her tongue, jammed her thumbs in her ears, wiggled her fingers at him, and then took off running. James lunged at his sister as she ran past him, sending his chair crashing to the floor. A second later Screech streaked around the corner with Spirit and Ribbon hot on her trail.

"This family is loco!" Gwen murmured to nobody but herself. "But I absolutely wouldn't trade them for anything!" Shaking her head, she got up from the table to start dinner.

 It didn't take long for Ribbon the Therapy Dog to work her magic on everyone at the nursing home. After just a few Saturday visits, the Border Collie managed to meet—and win over—each and every resident, as well as each and every staff member. Even Mr. Thomas, the administrator, who didn't particularly like dogs, was putty in her paws. Her visit was considered the highlight of each week.

In no time at all, Ribbon had achieved true rock star status at High Country Manor.

Excited about her dog's instant success, Allison hit on a plan as Valentine's Day approached. The first Saturday in February, she took her new digital camera with her on their visit and asked each resident if they would like their picture taken with Ribbon. To her delight, not one person said no. That evening she worked until midnight printing out all the pictures. Each showed a beaming elderly man or woman posing next to a smiling Border Collie.

"These are great!" raved Gwen when she saw the finished products. "Ribbon could be a dog model. She's very photogenic, and look how she gazes directly into the camera."

"Just another one of her many talents," observed Allison.

The next day Gwen helped her daughter insert each picture inside a colorful valentine card and write the resident's name on the envelope. Allison had noticed that many of the people loved to display photos on their bureaus and bedside tables. It was a way to keep family close, Allison supposed; and now that Ribbon was officially a part of their nursing home family, she wanted each of them to have a picture of their therapy dog to display.

Because Valentine's Day fell on a Thursday, Allison insisted to her mother they had to make a special visit to deliver the cards and photos on that day. Nurse Amy agreed it was fine for them to come after Allison got off from school.

"I want us to surprise everybody," Allison told her mother, as they drove to the nursing home. "This is going to be so much fun!" Ribbon, picking up on the excitement, had a hard time sitting still.

But the surprise was on them. All residents who weren't confined to bed were waiting for Allison, Gwen, and Ribbon in the large dining room when they arrived.

The chef had baked a gigantic heart-shaped chocolate cake with pink and red frosting for the humans, plus homemade heart-shaped dog biscuits for the rock star. Suspended from the ceiling was a banner sprinkled with hearts and cupids that read: "Ribbon and Allison, you have stolen our hearts!"

After all the valentines with photos had been passed out and lots of strawberry punch and cake had been consumed, Bob Jensen beckoned for Allison and Ribbon to come sit beside him at the piano in the front of the room. Allison settled herself on the piano bench and let Ribbon jump up beside her.

"It's time for a little music," Bob announced in a booming voice, causing everyone to stop talking. "This song is dedicated to this wonderful girl and her wonderful dog, who have made our lives so much sweeter." Then he began playing and singing the song "Let Me Call You Sweetheart," and before long every person in the room was swaying and singing along. Allison put her arms around Ribbon's chest and helped her sway to the music too.

Gwen and Amy stood in the back of the room, dabbing at their eyes with tissues. Looking around, they noticed they weren't the only ones doing that. Except for Ribbon's, there wasn't a dry eye in the place.

 As winter finally gave way to springtime in the Rockies, Allison and Ribbon would accompany some of the nursing home residents on short walks in the courtyard. If a resident became tired or out of breath, they'd find a bench to sit on and Ribbon would settle contentedly at the person's feet until they were ready to go again. The fresh mountain air and change of scenery seemed to give everyone a lift after being cooped up all winter long.

The Saturday before Easter, Allison had Ribbon don a pair of velvet bunny ears and then they set out to deliver candy-filled Easter baskets to each resident's room. When they arrived at Cora's bedside, the old woman's little girl giggle rang out at the sight of the Border Collie's new ears. "Well, I declare, you are cute as a bunny!" she said, reaching over with her good hand to pet the dog's head. Ribbon returned the favor by licking Cora's contracted hand with her warm tongue.

Easter Sunday dawned clear and bright. After they had attended Easter sunrise service and enjoyed a

breakfast of ham and cheese omelets and homemade hot cross buns, James agreed to help Allison take food to the O'Briens so Tim and Gwen could visit friends in Breckenridge. They loaded up Gwen's special orange-glazed pork roast, sweet potato casserole, and deviled eggs in the picnic basket and headed for the truck, Ribbon close at their heels. Even though the air was unusually warm for early April in the high country, Allison had put Ribbon's green knitted sweater on her so Mrs. O'Brien could see her wearing it.

"Please don't make any rude comments about Ribbon's sweater when we're at the O'Briens," Allison told her brother as they pulled out on to the highway. "It was very sweet of her to knit it, and all the residents at the nursing home comment on how cute Ribbon looks when she arrives wearing it, don't they girl?" Seated between them on the front seat, Ribbon looked from Allison to James and back to Allison.

Grinning, James reached over and cuffed the dog behind both ears. "Just don't let the goats see you in it, Ribbon. We don't want them laughing at you behind your back, now do we?"

Allison rolled her eyes as they drove on.

Mr. O'Brien propped open the door as the three-some came inside. "James, I think you must have grown at least a foot since we saw you last. Where have you been keeping yourself?"

"Well, when I'm not at school, I'm either helping Dad at the ranch or practicing with my band."

"So, you're a musician, are you? That's splendid!" Mr. O'Brien poured four glasses of lemonade and placed them on a tray while James and Allison unpacked the picnic basket. Meanwhile, Ribbon went to greet Mrs. O'Brien in the living room. They could hear the old woman cooing over her in a high-pitched voice.

"Come on, let's go in and see Mama. You know she was quite a singer in her day."

Mrs. O'Brien's eyes lit up when both youngsters leaned down to give her a peck on her rosy cheeks. "Well, what a treat! James, it's so good of you to come along with your sister and my precious Ribbon today."

Beckoning them to have a seat on the sofa, Mr. O'Brien handed Allison and James each a glass of lemonade. Ribbon stayed right by Mrs. O'Brien's recliner, leaning against her leg while the elderly woman patted her head over and over again.

"James is a musician, Mama. He says he has a band." Mr. O'Brien handed her a glass then sat down in his rocking chair.

"A musician!" She exclaimed. "How wonderful! What instrument do you play?"

"Guitar," James answered. "There's five of us in the band, and we play mostly rock and some country. When we played at school for the St. Patrick's Day dance, we even learned a few Irish folk songs."

"Did you learn 'When Irish Eyes Are Shining,' by any chance?" she asked eagerly.

"Yes. Do you know that one? Your husband says you are quite a singer."

"Aye, laddie," she answered in an exaggerated Irish brogue. "I was part of a trio called the Irish Lasses, and that song was our trademark for many years."

Allison looked at her brother and nudged his arm. "I have my guitar in the truck," he said. "Would you like me to play it while you sing?"

Mrs. O'Brien clapped her hands. "That would be loverly!"

"Let me get it," Allison said, standing up quickly. "I forgot to bring in something else from the truck." When she returned she was carrying Ribbon's green Delta Society vest, which she laid on Mrs. O'Brien's lap. "This is what Ribbon wears during her therapy visits at the nursing home. Look, it exactly matches the sweater you knit for her. It's almost like you had ESP!"

"Oh," Mrs. O'Brien grinned, eyes twinkling. "There was never any question what color I'd pick. We're Irish—so it just had to be green."

James chose that moment to start playing "When Irish Eyes Are Smiling," and Mrs. O'Brien picked up the tune in a clear soprano voice. As she sang, Allison and Mr. O'Brien exchanged smiles across the room. At the end of the song, Ribbon jumped up and planted a kiss on the singer's cheek, eliciting a squeal of delight.

"Ribbon obviously likes your singing voice," commented Allison. "But she knows not to give any kisses when she's in a work environment. That was part of her training."

"Well, I'm glad this house isn't a work environment because I love to get kisses from my precious Ribbon." The old woman put her arms around the Border Collie and hugged her tight.

James drained his glass of lemonade and stood up. "We better go and let you two get to your Easter dinner. It was nice to see you both again. Maybe I should come back to learn some more Irish songs before next St. Patrick's Day."

Mrs. O'Brien smiled broadly. "I'd love to teach you," she said, taking James' hand. "You three have really cheered me up and made this a wonderful Easter."

On the way home, James looked over at his sister and her dog snuggled together on the seat. "You know, you two do make a good therapy team. Mrs. O'Brien just lit up around you."

Allison sat up straight and looked at her big brother. "I'd say you worked a little magic yourself. Her Irish eyes were smiling when you played your guitar for her."

James ran his fingers through his unruly hair. "I admit that was kinda fun."

"Hey, wait a minute. I have an idea. Why don't you and your band play for the residents at High Country Manor sometime. I know they'd love it too."

James switched on the headlights in the gathering dusk. "Oh, I don't know, Sis. They might not like our kind of music."

"Oh, sure they would, wouldn't they, Ribbon?"

The dog barked in agreement.

As they rode the last couple of miles, all three occupants of the truck were lost in their own thoughts, and all three were smiling.

 One late May afternoon, Gwen received a call from her sister Eleanor in Denver. Auntie Ellie, as Allison and James called her, said she was working with a young burn patient at her hospital occupational therapy job and, unfortunately, was getting nowhere with her. She was hoping Allison and Ribbon might be able to help.

"I can't get this young girl to open up to me," Ellie explained, concern showing in her voice. "We've all tried to get through to her, but she's too traumatized by what she's been through to participate in her therapy."

"How do you think Allison and Ribbon can help?" Gwen asked.

There was a pause on the other end of the line as Ellie collected her thoughts. "Well, because Allison is about the same age as Katie, and because Ribbon is such a sensitive animal and has been through trauma of her own. I think maybe over time the two of them can make her feel safe enough to start coming out of her shell."

"OK, Ellie, let me talk it over with Allison and see what she thinks. School is out next week, so she will have more free time. We'll get back to you soon."

Gwen hung up and gazed out the kitchen window at the periwinkle blue columbines beginning to bloom beside the barn. She realized her daughter was beginning to blossom too. Allison's work with Ribbon at the nursing home had given her a confidence and maturity way beyond her years.

When Allison arrived home from school, Gwen poured a glass of milk and placed it on the table beside a plate of frosted chocolate pecan brownies she had just taken from the oven. "Sit down, honey. I want to talk something over with you."

Allison put down her backpack and sat down, reaching for a brownie with one hand and the milk with the other. "What's up?" she asked between gulps of the cold milk and bites of the warm brownie. Ribbon soon appeared at Allison's side, begging with her big brown eyes, but Allison shook her head no. "No chocolate for you, girl," she said firmly.

"Here, Ribbon, you deserve an afternoon snack too," Gwen said, opening the cupboard and bringing out a giant-sized rawhide bone, which the Border Collie quickly grasped between her teeth. Stretching out on the floor, the dog deftly maneuvered the bone into a vertical position between her front paws and began to methodically devour it.

"OK, Mom, shoot. Now that my belly's not growling anymore, you have my undivided attention."

Gwen sat down and took a brownie for herself. "Your Auntie Ellie called a little while ago. There is a young hospital patient where she works in Denver who is having a particularly hard time. The girl is about your age, and Ellie thinks maybe you and Ribbon might be able to help her."

Allison's green eyes widened. "She's my age? What happened to her? Why is she in the hospital?"

"Well, I don't have too many details. Ellie just said she's a burn patient and too traumatized right now to cooperate with her therapy. If you're interested, we can call Ellie tonight and find out more about..."

"Of course I'm interested, Mom!" Allison interrupted, her voice rising. "It must be so awful to be burned. If something like that happened to me, you'd want everybody to help me, wouldn't you?"

Ribbon looked up from her bone, sensing Allison's agitation.

"Of course, I'd want everyone to help you, sweetie. But if you and Ribbon sign on for this, you'd probably have to stay with Ellie in Denver for a while. With everybody's work schedule around here, it won't be possible to take you back and forth to the city every day. And it would also mean you would miss out on the camping trip to Rocky Mountain National Park with Charley and her family."

"Mom!" Allison waved her arms over her head, causing Ribbon to let out a whine. "I'm OK with all those things. Ribbon has been such a big hit at the nursing home with older people, imagine how awesome she'll be with a kid. Don't you remember her with that little child at the Halloween party? I know she'll be able to work a miracle with this girl. I just know it!"

Gwen reached across the table and took Allison's hands in hers. "All right, my enthusiastic daughter. I guess it's already settled then. We'll call your aunt tonight and go from there." She released Allison's hands and stood up. "Have I told you lately how much I admire your passion—not to mention your compassion?"

"Do you think Erma Bombeck would be proud of me and Ribbon?" Allison grinned, reaching for another brownie.

"I think she would be head over heels in love with both of you—just like I am."

"You know," Allison said, growing serious. "I've been thinking a lot about Erma's quote about using up every bit of talent we have before we die. I used to think that when some adult asked me what I wanted to do or be when I grow up, I had to pick one thing. Now I know that my answer can be: Lots of things!"

"That's right. That's what I love about what she's saying. It frees you to realize that you don't have to stay locked into one job or career all your life, you can try lots of things. And you can always have any number of hobbies that develop your other talents. Like your photography or your brother's music, for instance."

"Or your baking or Dad's sleigh restoring." Allison popped the last bite of brownie into her mouth and went to the sink to wash her gooey hands. She was careful to step over Ribbon, who had finished her own snack and was licking her front paws.

Gwen stood up and took off her apron. "Let's go out to the barn and tell your dad and James about the new challenge you two talented creatures are going to be taking on this summer."

By the time Allison had finished drying her hands, her dog was already waiting for them at the back door.

Chapter 21

On the last day of the school year, the cooks in the cafeteria prepared brown bag picnic lunches so all the teachers and students could eat outside on the school lawn. Allison and Charley carried their lunches over to a sunny picnic table and sat down, enjoying the warm breeze that ruffled Allison's ponytail and Charley's bouncy curls.

"I hope you're not mad that I can't go camping with you next week," Allison said, pulling a bag of chips and a ham sandwich from her bag. "My aunt thinks Ribbon and I might be able to help the burn patient I told you about. In my heart I know we can."

"Allison, I totally understand. I will miss you on our trip, but I think what you and Ribbon do is amazing. I'm positive you'll be able to help the patient." Charley took a sip of her chocolate milk. "And, besides, maybe you can come camping with us when my cousin from Pennsylvania comes later in the summer."

"Thanks for understanding. And because you're such a good buddy, you can have my piece of fruit." Allison handed Charley a bright red apple.

"You're just giving me it because it matches my hair," Charley quipped, and both girls broke into giggles. "Promise me you'll call me from Denver. I want to know everything that happens with your patient."

Traffic into Denver on Interstate 70 was heavy and Gwen was relieved when they finally turned off at her sister's exit. After stopping the car in Ellie's driveway, she helped Allison extract her duffel bag from the trunk, then lifted out a pan of homemade cinnamon buns, Ellie's favorite food, from the back seat.

Ellie welcomed Allison and Gwen each with a warm hug and then bent down to receive a kiss on the cheek from Ribbon. "What a lover you are!" she exclaimed, scratching the dog behind both ears. "I think you're just what the doctor ordered for my patient, Katie. She simply won't be able to resist all that doggy charm." Ribbon wagged her feathery tail and planted another kiss.

"Come on inside and relax." Ellie held open the front door as the threesome trooped into her cozy living room. Evidence of Ellie's two-year stint working at a hospital on the Navajo Reservation was everywhere. Brightly-colored Native American rugs were scattered over the hardwood floors and clay pots with eye-catching geometric designs lined the built-in shelves over the

Southwest-style fireplace. On the whitewashed walls hung poster-sized photographs of all kinds of exotic wildlife, taken by Ellie's husband Greg, a *National Geographic* photographer, who had been killed in a plane crash in Antarctica seven years earlier. And displayed in a large corner cupboard were carved wooden African masks and intricately woven baskets collected by Ellie's daughter, Rebecca, who was currently serving in the Peace Corps in Kenya.

Allison always loved being in this room, feeling like she was learning about the world and other cultures almost by osmosis.

"Sit down and put your feet up," Ellie said. "I'll get us something cold to drink after I put Allison's bag in Rebecca's old room. It'll be nice to have a kid around here again."

Allison and Gwen gratefully sank into the bright ethnic throw pillows on the leather sofa, and Ribbon let out a loud sigh as she sprawled at their feet.

Soon Ellie was back carrying a tray that held frosty glasses of root beer, a bright yellow plate with three of Gwen's homemade cinnamon buns on it, and a metal bowl of cool water for Ribbon, who didn't waste any time lapping it up. Ellie passed around napkins as Allison and her mother eagerly dove into the sticky pastries. Ribbon's begging paid off this time as Allison shared a chunk of her bun with her.

"Auntie Ellie, tell us about your patient, Katie. What exactly happened to her?"

"Well, Katie is a very talented musician. According to her parents, she has been taking piano lessons since she was only four years old and dreamed of being a concert pianist someday. But that dream ended two months ago when both of her hands were badly burned."

"Both her hands!" Allison exclaimed in horror. "Poor Katie!"

Gwen patted her daughter's knee. "How did it happen, Sis?"

"Well, apparently she was camping with her family in the foothills west of Denver. Her two-year-old brother stumbled near the campfire, and Katie grabbed him by his hooded sweatshirt to save him. The little boy came out completely unscathed, but, unfortunately, Katie's hands were burned in the process. She was immediately brought to the burn unit at the hospital where I work." Ellie took a sip of root beer before she continued. "Katie faces several surgeries in the months to come; but now that her burns are beginning to heal, we're trying to get her to participate in both physical and occupational therapy so her hands won't become contracted and stiff. But she's so traumatized and depressed that she won't even communicate with her own family, let alone the staff."

Allison sat very still, trying to imagine what it would be like to be in Katie's shoes. "Oh, Auntie Ellie, she must be so sad—and angry too. She probably thinks her life is over before it ever got started."

"Exactly!" Ellie replied. "I knew that you of all people—being Katie's age and having gone through Ribbon's accident—would understand what she is going through."

Gwen nodded in agreement and reached over to smooth Allison's hair. "You remember all those emotions you felt after Ribbon was hit by the car? Your dreams for her of winning the herding dog championship were dashed, but just look at what she's been able to accomplish since then."

At the mention of her name, Ribbon lifted her head then settled back into a napping position with a sigh, a smear of icing from the cinnamon bun high up on her long Collie nose.

Allison gently wiped Ribbon's icing off with a napkin, then looked from her mother to her aunt. "I think if I can tell Katie Ribbon's story—how she went from incredible herding dog to amazing therapy dog—Katie might eventually realize that she doesn't have to give up her dreams—just change them."

Ellie stood up and gave her niece and sister both a high five. "This kind of wisdom and dedication deserves a reward. I'm taking you ladies to my favorite steak house tonight for dinner. And we'll definitely bring Miss Ribbon home a doggy bag."

They all laughed as Ribbon got to her feet and lifted her right front paw straight up so Ellie could give her a high five too.

 After checking in with Mr. Connor, the hospital administrator, Ellie led Allison and Ribbon, wearing her official Delta Society vest and ID badge, to an elevator in the hospital lobby. When the elevator doors opened, Ribbon held back and Allison had to pull firmly on her leash to get her to go inside. "She's never been in an elevator before," Allison explained to her aunt as the doors closed. Ribbon looked around nervously, and when the elevator started to move upward, she crouched down on all fours as if holding on for dear life. She was the first one out when the doors re-opened.

Ellie leaned down and gave Ribbon a reassuring pat. "I can see riding the elevator is going to be the hardest part of your job, isn't it, girl?"

"I'm sure she'll get used to the elevator eventually," Allison said as they started down the corridor toward the nurse's station. "She adapts to things pretty quickly."

The young blonde nurse sitting at the desk jumped up to greet them when she realized a canine visitor was on the floor. "So this is the famous Ribbon we've been hearing about!" she exclaimed, coming around to pet the dog. "What a cutie you are!"

"This is Ribbon's owner, my niece Allison," Ellie said. "Allison and Ribbon are going to do their best to get through to Katie."

The nurse shook Allison's hand. "It's nice to meet you. We're all so worried about Katie. Thank you so much for coming to see her."

When they reached Katie's room, Ellie touched Allison's arm. "Let me go in first, so we don't overwhelm her," Ellie whispered. "I'll signal when it's OK to come in."

A young girl with shiny black hair to her shoulders and a sprinkling of freckles over her pale cheeks sat in a leather recliner staring out the window. She didn't even look up when Ellie bent down to talk to her. After a few minutes, Ellie waved for Allison and Ribbon to come in and moved a straight-backed chair over near Katie's chair for Allison to sit on. Ellie watched in wonder as Ribbon immediately positioned herself next to Katie's recliner and gently laid her head on the girl's lap.

Allison hesitated a moment, then said in a quiet voice, "My name is Allison and this is my dog, Ribbon. She's a Border Collie and she used to love to herd the goats and cattle on our ranch in the mountains; but, she was hit by a car and injured, so now she's learned to be a therapy dog."

Katie didn't say anything, but she did start to slowly stroke Ribbon's ruff with one of her hands, careful to keep it hidden beneath the dog's thick fur. Instinctively, Ribbon stayed very still and quiet, allowing the girl to go on petting her for the next few minutes. Allison noticed a tear roll down Katie's cheek as she continued to stare out the window.

Eventually, Ellie stood up and said, "Katie, we have to go now, but I'll bring Allison and Ribbon back to see you tomorrow. Is that OK?"

Katie nodded yes, before quickly pulling her hand back and shoving it under the blanket covering her legs. Ribbon backed up and went to Allison's side. "It was nice to meet you, Katie," Allison said softly. "We'll see you tomorrow."

When they reached the waiting room at the end of the hall, Ellie and Allison sat down to discuss what had just happened. "I'm really not sure how our visit went," Allison said. "What do you think, Auntie Ellie?"

"Well, you may not think we accomplished much in there, but actually it was quite a breakthrough for Katie," Ellie said, smiling at her niece. "Even though she didn't make eye contact or talk to us, she couldn't resist petting

Ribbon. That's the first time I've seen her voluntarily reach out with either hand."

"I noticed she didn't want us to see her hand. She put it right back under the blanket when we got up to leave," Allison observed. "I guess I'd feel that way, too."

"Yes, that's a natural reaction. But she did use that hand for the first time. And another thing—she began to cry a little today. Up until now she's bottled up her feelings deep inside her. She needs to be able to let them out in order to begin to heal emotionally."

"So it was a good start then." Allison looked down at her dog sitting patiently at her feet. "Ribbon is beginning to work her magic, isn't she?"

"She certainly is. Animals have an amazing ability to put people at ease. They don't care if we're not perfect—they love us unconditionally."

The following day, Katie was lying in bed with the covers pulled up to her chin and her back to the door when the threesome arrived at her room. A game show was on the TV, but Katie didn't seem to be watching it. Ribbon made her way around the bed, stood up on her hind legs, then stretched her body across Katie's, resting her crooked front leg on the girl's shoulder. As Katie straightened out her body under the sheets, she noticed Ribbon's injured leg and gently cradled it in both her hands. "Poor puppy," she cooed. "Poor puppy."

Just then, the young blonde nurse beckoned to Ellie and Allison from the hall. "We'll be right back, Katie," Ellie called over her shoulder as they left the room.

The nurse asked if they would stop in the waiting room on their way out so a little boy there could get to meet Ribbon. "Of course!" Allison answered immediately. "Ribbon loves little kids—she even lets them ride her sometimes."

Ellie and Allison turned back to go into Katie's room, but what they saw stopped them in their tracks. Katie was hugging Ribbon tightly with both arms, her head was buried in the dog's soft fur, and she was sobbing as if her heart would break.

The Border Collie stayed motionless until the girl's sobs completely subsided. When Katie finally raised her head and dried her tears on the sleeve of her hospital gown, Ellie and Allison took their cue to move closer to the bed. "I think I got your dog all wet," Katie smiled weakly in Allison's direction.

"That's OK," Allison smiled back. "She's used to it. She's absorbed a lot of my tears too, haven't you, Ribbon?"

Ribbon answered with a quick bark.

"Thank you for bringing her," Katie said, looking first at Allison and then at Ellie. "Will all of you please come visit me again tomorrow?"

Ribbon barked again as she backed away from the bed and went to stand between Allison and Ellie. "That would be a definite yes," laughed Allison. "We'll be here."

Chapter 23

Over the next week, Ellie, Allison, and Ribbon made daily visits to Katie's hospital room, and each day Katie opened up a little more. One afternoon she asked about the details of Ribbon's accident as she carefully stroked the dog's injured leg with her own injured hand. When Allison told her how Ribbon had run into traffic to save one of the goats, Katie took the dog's face between her hands and exclaimed, "Why, Ribbon you were a hero!"

"Yes, she was," Allison agreed. She looked over at Ellie and then said, "Auntie Ellie tells me you were a hero too."

"Me? A hero?" Katie looked puzzled.

"Yes, she told me you rescued your little brother from stumbling into a campfire. My social studies teacher taught us that a hero is someone who willingly puts himself in harm's way to save someone else. That's exactly what you and Ribbon both did."

Katie was silent for a long time. She brushed her long dark hair away from her face and then spoke in a hushed voice. "I guess I've been focusing so much on the negative—what I've lost—that I forgot about the positive—what I still have. I love my brother more than anything in the world, and he's just fine."

"Thanks to you," Ellie pointed out.

"Yes, thanks to you," Allison reiterated.

A rosy blush crept over Katie's usually pale cheeks. "I guess you're right."

"Hey, I have an idea!" Allison stood up and walked to the side of the bed. "Do you think your little brother would like to meet Ribbon?"

"Are you kidding? He loves anything with four legs. And he would definitely fall in love with Ribbon—just like I did."

"Do your parents ever bring him to the hospital to visit you?" Allison asked.

"He's been away visiting our grandparents in Nebraska, but he's coming home this weekend."

"Well, we're going home for the weekend—Ribbon and I visit a nursing home on Saturdays near where we live—but we'll be back next week."

"Good! I can't wait for Jimmy to meet Ribbon," Katie said, petting the dog with both hands.

"Is Jimmy's real name James?"

"Yes, why?"

"Because I have a brother James too—only he's six years older than me. I love him more than anything in the world, too, but of course I'd never tell him that. It would just go to his head."

"I know just what you mean," Katie giggled.

Ellie smiled to herself as she watched the two girls interact and bond. Ribbon and Allison had succeeded in breaking through Katie's shell. Now it was time to push Katie to get serious about the therapy she so desperately needed. It wouldn't be easy for Katie, but Ellie was confident the healing had already begun.

 Once she agreed to cooperate with her therapists, Katie bravely pushed through the pain to do everything they asked her to do. As she performed all the hand exercises over and over again, her misshapen fingers grew stronger and more flexible. And, as her physical condition improved, so did her mood and her confidence. After only two weeks, her doctors decided to discharge her from the hospital and switch her to outpatient therapy.

Allison and Ribbon continued to visit Katie in the outpatient therapy department of the hospital whenever Allison's mother had a day off from work to drive them to Denver. It didn't take long for the Border Collie to become the darling of all the patients and therapists there, as she went from person to person dispensing her doggy charms. They soon found out that Ribbon the Therapy Dog knew a thing or two about therapy.

One day, Allison, Gwen, and Ribbon arrived to find Katie so excited she could hardly sit still. "We have a surprise for Ribbon today," Katie announced, unself-consciously clapping her hands together. "Come here, girl. These are for you." The dog walked over and sat at the girl's feet as Katie picked up a collar and a leash made of beautifully-woven sturdy dark green ribbon that exactly matched Ribbon's Delta Society vest. After fastening the collar around Ribbon's neck and hooking the leash on the collar, Katie proudly led her around the room to show off her new accessories.

"Katie, the collar and leash are awesome! Did you make them yourself?" Allison asked in disbelief.

"Yes, it was hard at first, but very good therapy for my hands to braid them, and now I'm teaching all the other patients here how to do it."

A woman in a purple outfit seated in a wheelchair shouted from across the room, "It's fun once you get the hang of it."

"There's no stopping us now," chimed in a stroke patient wearing overalls, who held up a partially finished collar with his good hand.

Just then Ellie appeared in the doorway, walked over to where her sister and niece were sitting, and flashed Katie the thumbs up sign.

"You mean you got the go-ahead?" Katie asked her.

"Yes, ma'am, it's a go!"

"What's a go?" asked Allison, looking from Katie to Ellie.

"You tell her, Katie," Ellie smiled.

"Well, we all came up with an idea as a group that we could sell the collars and leashes we make to raise money for the Delta Society so more dogs like Ribbon could be trained to be therapy dogs."

Unable to control her excitement, Ellie interrupted. "And I just received the official OK from hospital administration to have a one-day Therapy Dog Fundraiser here at the hospital in the fall. In addition to selling the collars and leashes, we'll have lots of food booths and other vendors, plus pet contests and games for the kids. We'll make it a dog-friendly event and invite other therapy dogs from the area. What do you think?"

Allison hugged Katie. Gwen hugged Ellie. And everyone in the room took turns hugging Ribbon.

 Between nursing home visits, trips to Denver, and an occasional camping outing with Charley, the remainder of the summer passed quickly for Allison. It wasn't long before school had started again and the aspen leaves began to cast their golden glow in the high country.

The long-awaited day of the Therapy Dog Fundraiser turned out to be clear but especially chilly. Rising early, Allison and her parents dressed warmly, then gathered everything for their trip to Denver: camera equipment, a large cooler stacked with Gwen's cinnamon apple pies to sell, and Allison's backpack containing Ribbon's water dish, green leash, and Delta Society vest. After all had been stowed in the trunk of the car, Allison opened the car door when the guest of honor, decked out in her hand-knit green sweater, appeared on the scene. "After you, Your Highness," she said, ushering the Border Collie into the back seat with a flourish.

"Everybody ready for takeoff?" Tim asked, starting the engine. He chuckled as he noticed Allison's and Ribbon's two smiling faces in the rearview mirror.

Soon they were on Interstate 70 heading east to Denver. While they rode, Gwen passed out blueberry muffins still warm from the oven and Styrofoam cups of hot chocolate. Allison secretly shared her muffin with Ribbon, then stretched out on the back seat with her dog at her side. She felt happy and secure as she gazed at the familiar bright blue of the Colorado sky through the car window and heard her parents' soft chatter from the front seat.

Cupping her hand around Ribbon's good ear, she whispered, "It's been over a year since your accident, girl, and we've definitely come a long way, baby."

Ribbon planted a sloppy kiss on Allison's upturned nose before settling in for a doggy nap that lasted the whole way to Denver.

After finding a lucky parking spot near the front door of the hospital, Tim helped unload everything from the car and led the way into the hospital lobby. When he noticed a large poster advertising today's Therapy Dog Fundraiser, he set down the cooler and reached for his daughter, hugging her to his chest. "I can see the money we spent on that digital camera was money well spent. This poster is absolutely beautiful, honey."

Gwen tugged on Allison's ponytail and smiled proudly as they all studied the poster. Allison had

photographed Ribbon wearing her green collar, leash, and vest, with her injured leg raised in greeting. She was also wearing her Border Collie smile.

"I had a very good model," Allison said, stooping down to pat Ribbon's head before they all continued down the hall.

Outside in the courtyard, chaos reigned. People were running from booth to booth, putting finishing touches on signs, setting up folding chairs, and unloading food. Tim and Gwen found the pie booth and began to unpack the cooler. Allison scanned the growing crowd and finally spotted Katie sitting with two other therapy patients at a long table covered with green collars and leashes laid out in neat rows. Allison and Ribbon made their way over to the table just as Ellie arrived from the opposite direction.

"I have some exciting news for you two young ladies," Ellie announced, slipping her cell phone into her pocket. "I just got a call from a reporter at the *Rocky Mountain News*. He is interested in interviewing both of you later today, after the festivities get started."

Allison and Katie looked at each other in amazement. "Why us?" they asked in unison.

But they never got an answer because Ellie's cell phone rang at that moment and she went scurrying off across the courtyard to help another therapist set up some sound equipment.

"Look, here come my folks!" Katie pointed as her parents and brother headed in their direction. When Jimmy spied Ribbon, he got so excited he waved his chubby little arms then fell flat on his face. Within a few seconds he was up on his feet again and happily yelling, "Doggy, here doggy!" as Allison brought Ribbon over for him to pet. Ribbon didn't seem to mind at all as Jimmy patted and hugged her and even tumbled on top of her.

"I swear that's the most good-natured dog I've ever met," Katie's father told Allison, as they watched the dog and toddler roll around on the grass. "Jimmy hasn't stopped talking about Ribbon since you brought her to Katie's hospital room to meet him."

"She is really good and patient with little kids," Allison commented.

"And with big kids, too," Katie interjected, pointing at herself.

"And goats and older people and…" Allison stopped mid-sentence when she noticed Amy, the nurse from High Country Manor, pushing Bob Jensen in a wheelchair across the walkway. "Oh my gosh! Speaking of older people, there's Mr. Jensen from the nursing home where Ribbon makes therapy visits. I can't believe he came the whole way here. Excuse me, I need to take Ribbon over to greet him."

Katie's father hoisted Jimmy up in his arms, saying "Doggy has to go now," as Allison led Ribbon away.

Bob Jensen's eyes lit up when he saw Allison and Ribbon coming toward him. "There are my two sweethearts!" he chortled, giving both a hug. "Thanks to Nurse Amy here, I get to share your big day—and to bring something along from the residents at the nursing home." From his vest pocket, he produced a long sealed white envelope and handed it to Allison. "Go ahead. Open it, sweetheart. It's from all of us."

Allison's big green eyes widened as they focused on the check made out to the Delta Society in the amount of $250. "This is wonderful!" Allison said softly, trying to choke back her emotions.

Amy put her arms around Allison's shoulders. "Every one of the residents contributed whatever they could. It's their way of saying "thank you" to you and Ribbon for bringing such joy into their lives."

More surprise visitors appeared just as Allison was returning to the leash table after giving the nursing home check to the hospital administrator. Her brother James and Spirit, both wearing hand-knit green sweaters, came striding across the courtyard with Mr. and Mrs. O'Brien following along behind.

"There's my precious Ribbon!" Mrs. O'Brien's high-pitched voice rang out loud and clear above the noise the crowd. Ribbon went over to give the old woman a greeting, careful not to topple her walker in the process.

Allison walked over to the elderly couple, exclaiming how wonderful it was for them to come. "James was nice enough to bring us in his truck," Mr. O'Brien said, beaming. "We wouldn't have missed this for the world."

Mrs. O'Brien stopped fussing over Ribbon long enough to give Allison an enthusiastic hug. "The most splendid thing happened when we were coming down the corridor inside the hospital," she said. "A lady with a Yorkshire Terrier and another lady with a Poodle noticed Spirit's sweater, and when I told them I had knit it, they immediately wanted to order sweaters for their dogs."

"That's great! What did you say?" Allison stole a glance at James, who was looking very sheepish.

"I told them, yes, I'd make them and donate the money I charge them for the sweaters to the Delta Society in honor of my precious Ribbon."

"And I betcha she gets a lot more orders before the day's over," Mr. O'Brien said proudly, patting his wife's hand. "That'll keep her busy for quite a while."

Allison bent down to pet Spirit, and James knelt beside her. "I suppose you've noticed my sweater," he whispered.

"How could I miss it, brother dear," she whispered back. "Aren't the goats going to laugh at you behind your back when you wear it at the ranch?"

"It's not the goats I'm worried about—it's the other guys in the band."

Allison ruffled her brother's unruly hair and giggled. "Actually, I think it was very sweet of you to wear it out in public. And it was also very sweet of you to bring Mr. and Mrs. O'Brien here today. I always knew you were a big softie."

"I do have my moments," James replied.

When she stood up, Allison glimpsed a mop of curly red hair over near the food booths and knew it could only belong to her pal Charley. She started off in that direction but was intercepted by Ellie, who came up behind her. "Allison, you and Ribbon are wanted up on stage. They're going to be making some announcements soon."

"But I want to introduce my friend Charley to Katie."

"You'll have to do that later, honey," Ellie replied. "They need you on stage right away. I'll see you later." With that she disappeared into the crowd.

Allison and Ribbon made their way to the makeshift stage that had been set up at the north end of the courtyard. Mr. Connor, the hospital administrator, was waiting for them and ushered them to a row of chairs at the side of the stage.

Katie arrived a minute later. "Do you know why we're up here? Your aunt just told me to hurry and come to the stage."

"Not a clue," Allison answered. "She told me the same thing."

Just then, a loud screech emitted from the sound system, sending Ribbon under Allison's chair, her front paws covering her ears. A moment later, Mr. Connor's voice could be heard, asking everyone for their attention. "Ladies and Gentlemen, before we continue with the day's festivities, the hospital staff would like to recognize three special individuals who made today's Therapy Dog Fundraiser possible." He waited for the background noise to die down, then continued, "Our first individual is a brave young lady who was admitted to our burn unit after rescuing her younger brother from a fire. Thanks to the intervention of an amazing therapy dog, she was able to heal emotionally and go on to participate in the necessary physical and occupational therapy that would eventually help her physical wounds to heal. The beautiful green ribbon collars and leashes on sale today are her original creations. With the help of other therapy patients, these items are being made and sold to help the Delta Society continue its wonderful mission of training and certifying therapy animals for hospitals, rehab clinics, and nursing homes throughout the nation."

Applause and cheers broke out, and Mr. Connor again waited for the noise to subside. "Katie Wilson, please come forward. We have something to give to you to thank you for all your perseverance and hard work."

Katie hugged Allison and Ribbon before she crossed the stage to receive a huge bouquet of yellow roses. More applause and cheers rang out and lasted for several minutes.

Mr. Connor returned to the microphone. "And now for our second individual. She, too, is an amazing young lady who never gives up. When the injuries her beloved Border Collie sustained in a car accident dashed all hopes of winning the herding dog championships, this young girl found another outlet for her dog's energy and talents. After passing the Delta Society Pet Partners evaluation test with flying colors, this dog-handler team went to work immediately at High Country Manor in Summit County. Proof of the impact they have had at that nursing home is right here in my pocket." He paused and pulled out the check. "This is a $250 check made out to the Delta Society—it was collected by all the residents at the nursing home to show their love and gratitude."

As the crowd began to applaud again, Mr. Connor said, "Allison Colby, please come forward. We have something to give to you to thank you for all your hard work and dedication."

Allison removed Ribbon's leash from her collar and told her to "stay" before she crossed the stage to receive a huge bouquet of red roses. Again the cheers and applause lasted several minutes.

Mr. Connor cleared his throat and then went on. "And now for our third individual. Frankly, she is something of a thief. With her quiet instincts, comforting presence, and irresistible smile, she has managed to steal the hearts of everyone she has come into contact with at this hospital." He paused to hold up the Therapy Dog Fundraiser poster. "She is truly the poster dog for this wonderful event today. Ribbon Colby, please come forward. We have something to give to you to thank you for all your hard work and inspiration."

At Allison's hand signal, Ribbon stood and crossed the stage to receive a huge cellophane bag of doggy treats tied with a curly green ribbon. This time, the cheers and applause that rang out were especially deafening and included a few loud barks from the other canines in the courtyard.

As Katie, Allison, and Ribbon walked to the center of the stage to have their picture taken by the *Rocky Mountain News* photographer, the sight of all the dear, familiar faces beaming at them from the front of the crowd sent Allison's heart soaring. Her father and mother, James and Spirit in their green sweaters, Auntie Ellie, nurse Amy and Bob Jensen, the O'Briens, Charley and her parents, and Katie's mother and father, supporting a bouncing Jimmy on his shoulders. She made a mental note to take a group picture of everyone later so she would have a lasting reminder of this amazing day.

After the photographer had finished taking multiple shots of the three celebrities, Ellie joined them on stage to introduce them to reporter Andy Watson. "It's an honor to meet all three of you," he said. "I just need to ask you a few questions, if that's OK." When Allison and Katie nodded yes, he led them to the chairs at the side of the stage and took out a notebook and pen as Ribbon stretched out at their feet.

Andy's first questions were about Ribbon. Allison filled in all the details of how her dog had transitioned from herder to healer, as she put it.

"From herder to healer, I like that phrase. That will make a catchy headline for the article." The reporter wrote in his notebook, then turned his attention to Katie. At his prompting, Katie described how Ribbon had managed to break down her defenses and make her realize that despite her injuries—like the dog herself—she still had a future and a lot to offer the world.

"So," Andy said, closing his notebook, "this is basically a story about the incredible healing power of animals, isn't it?"

Ribbon sat up and smiled, placing her crooked front leg on the reporter's knee, which caused him to smile back at her and stroke her leg gently with both hands.

Allison leaned over to pat her dog's head. "Despite her disabilities—or maybe because of them—Ribbon is still the best Border Collie in Colorado, aren't you, girl?"

"No, she isn't," Katie said, shaking her head.

Allison and Andy both looked at Katie in disbelief. Even Ribbon cocked her head at Katie, her ears in an upright position.

Grinning, Katie paused dramatically. "She's the best Border Collie in the whole world!"

About the Author/Illustrator

Lyn Bezek, a Registered Nurse and writer from Pueblo, Colorado, believes you can be lots of different things when you grow up. This is her second book in the Children of Colorado series.

Su Hand is also a Registered Nurse and an artist from Pueblo. She has been painting since her mother put a brush in her hand at age six. She had great fun illustrating *Ribbon*, her first children's book.